CRUSHED

GOLD HOCKEY #18

ELISE FABER

CRUSHED
BY ELISE FABER
Newsletter sign-up

GOLD HOCKEY SERIES

***Gold Hockey* (all stand alone)**
Blocked
Backhand
Boarding
Benched
Breakaway
Breakout
Checked
Coasting
Centered
Charging
Caged
Crashed
A Gold Christmas
Cycled
Caught
Cap
Covered
Crushed
Changed

GOLD CAST OF CHARACTERS

Heroes and Heroines:

Brit Plantain (Blocked) — first female goalie in the NHL, loves boy bands

Stefan Barie (Blocked) — captain of the Gold

Sara Jetty (Backhand) — artist and figure skater

Mike Stewart (Backhand) —defenseman for the Gold, romance guru

Blane Hart (Boarding) — center for the Gold, number 22

Mandy Shallows (Boarding) — trainer and physical therapist

Max Montgomery (Benched) — defensemen for the Gold, giant nerd

Angelica Shallows (Benched) — engineer at RoboTech, also a giant nerd

Blue Anderson (Breakaway) — top forward in the league and for the Gold

Anna Hayes (Breakaway) — Max's former nanny, no relation to Kevin Hayes

Rebecca Stravokraus (Breakout) — Gold publicist, makes killer brownies, known at PR-Rebecca

Kevin Hayes (Breakout) — forward for the Gold, no relation to Anna Hayes

Rebecca Hallbright (Checked) — nutritionist for the Gold, plethora of delicious vegan recipes, known as Nutrionist-Rebecca

Gabe Carter (Checked) — doctor, head trainer for the Gold

Calle Stevens (Coasting) — assistant coach for the Gold, former national team member

Coop Armstrong (Coasting) — talented forward on the Gold, addicted to historical romance audiobooks

Mia Caldwell (Centered) — 5th degree black belt, brings the snark

Liam Williamson (Centered) — Gold forward finding his love for the game, charming and pushy in equal measures

Charlotte Harris (Charging) — new Gold GM, hates losing and the game Chubby Bunny

Logan Walker (Charging) — defensemen for the Gold, skills include: cockiness and being able to buy presents that make Charlotte squirm

Dani Eastbrook (Caged) — video coach for the Gold, tech nerd, could fix your computer in a flash, shy

Ethan Korhonen (Caged) — forward for the Gold, killer power play skills, known as Big Juicy Brain

Fanny Douglas (Crashed) — silver medalist, skating coach for the Gold

Brandon Cunningham (Crashed) — brown curls, penchant for hallways, Kaydon Lewis's agent

Kaydon Lewis (Cycled)— yummy stubble, great with kids, doesn't mind a little snot

Scarlett Andrews (Cycled)—quiet, perfectionist, resembled Bambi on ice

Charlie Andrews (Caught)— Scarlett's brother and total romantic

Kacee (Caught)— the woman inside the giant Gold nugget

Joshua Webb (Cap)— tall, smart, and handsome, the newest captain of the Gold

Jess White (Cap)— assistant video coach and obsessed with a certain new captain

Benjamin Roberts (Covered)— snarky, smart, and dipping a toe where he shouldn't

Jordyn Webb (Covered)— single mom and Josh's sister

Will Johansson (Crushed)— smart, sensitive, and likes Shirley Temples

Lily Cartwright (Crushed)— sports psychologist and obsessed with fluffy pancakes

Additional Characters:

Bernard — head coach

Richie — equipment manager

Dan Plantain — Brit's brother

Diane Barie — Stefan's mom

Pierre Barie — Stefan's dad, owner of the Gold

Spence — former goalie, married to Monique, daughter Mirabel

Monique — married to Spence, former model

Mirabel — daughter of Spence and Monique

Mitch — Sara's boss

Allison and Sean — Blane's parents

Pascal — Devon Scott's security lead

Roger Shallows — Mandy's dad

Grant and Megan — Devon's parents

ONE

LILY

She was tired of this shit.

Like *beyond* tired of it.

Tired of her boss standing less than a foot from her, his taller body bent so that he could better yell at her, blood vessels having burst in his eyes, spittle flying in tiny, disgusting globs that luckily hadn't yet splattered against her cheeks.

Thankful for her glasses providing eye protection when one of those gross orbs hit the lens.

Bile in her throat.

Her stomach churning.

A year ago, she might have thought she would throw up.

But she'd endured all manner of things in the last three-hundred-sixty-odd days. A little spit on her glasses was the least of her concern.

Same as the screaming.

For the last six months or so, she'd been able to go full-on Charlie Brown—*whun-whun, whun-whun, whun-whun.* So, the yelling didn't bother her.

It was *what* he was yelling about.

It was the fact that the people she was supposed to be looking after, helping, *protecting* were seen as a commodity without feelings or the chance to make mistakes or—

"And if she doesn't get her fucking head together," Zack thundered, drawing Lily's hearing into focus, "you can tell her that she's off the goddamned team!"

Then—as was his modus operandi—he didn't wait for a response or confirmation. He just straightened and stormed out of her office, slamming the door behind him and setting her trio of tiny cacti rattling on the small shelf she'd mounted on the same wall.

One of these days, it would crash to the ground.

Broken. Unsalvageable. Adorable ceramic pots ravaged. Gone forever. Never to be pieced back together.

And *that* was a painful reminder of—

Exhaling sharply, she tucked the memory away and then turned back to her computer, beginning to pull files and compile resources. Leslie was scheduled to be in Lil's office in just over an hour, and Lily would be ready for any scenario, any need, anything that she might require.

Anything to help her young athlete get back on track, despite the shit that Zack was pulling.

Because Lily wouldn't fail her.

Blowing out another breath—since that was the only way to get rid of the burning in the back of her throat, the tension swirling in her stomach, the agonizing regret that she hadn't done enough—she focused and...*worked.*

It was what she was good at.

What she was *best* at.

So, when Leslie came in an hour later, she was ready.

And then, when Veronica and Chelsea came in afterward, eyes red and glassy, posture shrunken in a way that Lily knew instantly was strictly because of Zack, she wanted to scream and throw something at her stupid trio of cacti. To shatter the pretty porcelain exteriors herself, to destroy the beauty before the world did.

But...she was a fixer.

She fought for it, tried her best to be that glue.

It just...didn't always work.

Today, though, it did. Something she was thankful for when she saw the light creep back into Leslie's eyes, her love and determination for the sport sliding back into her as their session went on. Even as Lily pushed away the fact that she'd had that thought before. She *had* to. It was the only way forward, the only way to escape the labyrinth of the memories, the monster of her past. Focus on work, on Veronica and Chelsea, on the fact that they'd become roadkill for Zack as well and needed her.

Then, hours later, when her office was empty and Zack's car had left the parking lot, she did what she'd done for the last eleven and a half months—which was exactly how long it had taken for her to recognize Zack for what he was.

Which, okay, she'd known what he was within a few seconds of meeting him—a creep—but he'd been on his best behavior for those two weeks, so she'd ignored her instincts, had dismissed the red flags waving in her belly.

Because then the shine had come off.

And—she wasn't a pushover, wasn't a woman to let wrongs continue without doing her best to right them—she reported him. For the first time. But not the last.

Even though it didn't do anything, didn't *change* anything.

Didn't make one bit of difference.

Just like she reported the bruises she saw on Leslie's arm that day.

Shaped like fingertips. Five of them. Lily had been able to count them.

Which was why—this time—she didn't just report Zack's emotional abuse to their parent organization and Zack's boss and the president of the committee, who was supposed to watch out for these young athletes. She didn't just send another email to Leslie's and Chelsea's and Veronica's parents.

She also reported those bruises to the police.

Two

In fairness, she hadn't expected it to all blow up like it had.

Reports erased from the organization's internal system, files shredded, parents paid off with promises of better opportunities for their extremely gifted young athletes if only they would lend their support to the coaches.

Parasites.

Living their dreams through children.

Including Leslie's parents.

Getting hurt is sometimes part of the process.

A direct quote from the Parents of the Year in response to Lily's last email to them.

That had assuaged Lily's guilt—or some of it, anyway. She was a mandatory reporter. She knew she had a duty to protect her kids. She knew Leslie's parents wouldn't.

She'd failed her girls once.

She wouldn't fail them again, wouldn't ignore the signs, pretend that things would get better.

So, Lily had continued doing her job, continued advocating and protecting and bringing physical and digital copies of *every-*

thing home in the days that had followed her report to the police (and only *days* because she'd known her time in her position was limited once she'd called the non-emergency line). Those copies... well, they'd both become instrumental and a huge issue for her legally. The only reason she had them at all was because, from the moment *her* parents had heard about Zack and the shitshow that was supposed to have been her dream job, they'd had Lily's back. A place to vent. A sounding board of workplace experience and advice. Advice that had saved her.

CYA

Cover. Your. Ass.

Her mom was an HR higher-up in a Fortune 500 company. She was great at her job, experienced, and her guidance had saved Lily—at least legally.

It was technically against the rules—something the organization had fired her for when the police showing up to investigate the bruises had prompted an internal inquiry—her taking those files, bringing the copies of her reports home. But they'd been the backbone of the case that was currently playing out on national television, so much so that her lawyer had managed to get her whistleblower status.

Her legal problems solved.

No ramifications for taking the files.

And thankfully, being a whistleblower meant that her name was left out of it.

At least in the public sphere.

The back channels, though, the powerful humans that oversaw the profit machine that was professional sport?

They knew.

They knew she'd reported and continued reporting even though it had done jack shit. They knew she'd then finally seized the opportunity of something physical—and fuck, that made her sound almost as bad as the powers that had kept Zack coaching—because she'd taken advantage of a child's pain, a child's bruises, and brought the police in. Had sneakily snapped cell phone photos because Lily knew that Leslie wouldn't consent to her bruises being documented otherwise. And then...Lily had used them. Had given them to the police, along with copies of every single line of text she'd smuggled out.

Thankfully, the detective had taken her seriously.

And the investigation that had followed had imploded a powerhouse of American sports. Because the subsequent glare of the media spotlight on what had formerly been seen as a crowning jewel in the country's gold medal hopes had been blinding.

Dreams dashed. Coaches fired. Sponsorships pulled.

Eyes looking closely, searching with a fine-toothed comb through many other facets of the sport. Of *many* sports.

She'd started that.

Thus, she'd become persona non grata.

As in, no job. No bites from the postings she'd submitted to. No résumés requested or followed up on. No...*nothing*.

Just her and an inbox brimming with angry emails from parents whose children were scrambling to continue fulfilling those dreams (or rather, more often their dreams, and only occasionally their child's) by finding different places to train.

Just her and the knowledge that she'd done the right thing, even if it left her feeling like a user.

Even though it had all gone wrong since.

Even though—her gaze drifted to the photograph on her shelf —it didn't feel like she'd done nearly enough.

Didn't do it *soon* enough.

Didn't—

She sighed, slammed her laptop closed, blocking out the job posting site.

The issue with finding another place to work was that her job was specialized. She'd worked and inched and clawed her way into her position—volunteer to intern to a full-time paid position. That was interspersed with years of education and more volunteering and more...

Clawing. Inching. Schmoozing.

Making the right connections. Putting in the correct hours.

Taking the proper classes. Working with the professors who would help propel her forward.

The industry was predominantly connection-based. A who's who of associations and ties and...

Word-of-mouth.

Which meant she'd fucked up.

If she wanted to keep doing what she was doing, that was.

There wasn't a giant pool of positions she could apply for to begin with, and with her unknown-in-the-public, but-known-in-the-background role, she wasn't going to get any positions through the channels she'd used before.

She was a sports psychologist.

There weren't an infinite number of professional teams and organizations who had her position on their payroll, and those who did typically already had that role filled. She could go back to volunteering, but she liked to—*shrug*—do things like eat and stream bad reality TV and splurge on the occasional pair of very expensive socks.

Volunteering didn't pay the bills.

She *could* open her own practice.

But it wasn't like there were a plethora of professional athletes in her neighborhood—not without the connection of a team.

And anyone making the big bucks probably had enough resources to fly someone in or travel to someone they wanted to work with. Or, hell, already had a person on staff they could turn to.

Anyway, what was so special about her that they would want to go out of their way to work with *her?*

She was...

Her gaze flicked back to the photograph on her shelf, heart squeezing, stomach churning.

She wasn't so sure there was *anything* special about her—at least nothing special enough to propel someone to fly across the country to sit for an hour on a dumpy couch, in a crappy office (because volunteering also didn't pay for a fancy office, or even things like a set of leather love seats).

Ikea all the way, baby.

Her dad could help her with prints for the wall, she supposed. He was a working artist, but he'd cut his only daughter a good deal.

And they'd be good.

Her mom had taught Lily to CYA. Her dad, on the other hand, would take the flurry of emotions tangled in her heart and mix them together, using paint and canvas and whatever scraps he might find that would bring texture and life and—

"Right, Lil," she whispered, rubbing a hand over her face.

She was losing it.

Even if she did manage to scrape enough money together to start her own practice, she certainly wouldn't draw in professional athletes. Lil would probably end up with a revolving couch of pickleball enthusiasts, all of whom would spend their sessions lamenting about their partner's lack of racket etiquette.

That seemed like a fate worse than death.

And yes, even psychologists bartered in drama and hyperbole.

Hell, with all they heard and worked through and advised on, they might exist solely in a world of hyperbole.

Sighing, knowing she was still being ridiculous, but giving herself the space to be it for a few more hours anyway, she snagged the remote, wrapped her favorite fluffy blanket around her legs, and hit the power button.

Trash TV would cure all.

Or, at least, it would remind her that her life wasn't the biggest dumpster fire around.

But just as she'd begun to really soak in all of those on-screen dumpster fires (of all sizes), her doorbell rang.

Worry down her spine, balling her intestines into a taut, twisting knot.

She didn't like surprise visitors.

Mostly because, in the last few months, they'd ranged from

the police to a process server (before her attorney had gotten her out of her legal trouble) to angry parents. Mostly because she was worried someone would let her name slip and then it wouldn't be a police officer or someone serving her scary papers littered with words she didn't understand.

She worried it would be a reporter.

And she would be swept right along into the surge of media coverage.

There was nothing that people loved more than tearing down their heroes.

She didn't consider herself one. She'd done her job. It had helped some, been too late for one, but God knew she didn't want people picking through the wreckage of her life, talking to ex-boyfriends or finding someone she might have slighted in middle school.

Lil was a good person.

But she wasn't perfect.

So...she hoped to God it wasn't a reporter as she carefully tossed back the blanket, muted the TV, and moved to her door.

A breath as she peeked through the sidelight.

Another as she tried to place the familiar face that was staring back.

A third as she decided that even if it *was* a reporter, at least the woman standing on her porch seemed to have a nice smile.

And a patient demeanor as Lil stared dumbly for a few more seconds before her brain kicked back in and she remembered she'd actually have to *open* her door and speak to the woman in order to solve the mystery of her porch interloper.

"Right," she whispered.

Lily flicked the lock, tugged open the door.

"Hi, Lily," the woman said, sticking out her hand, encasing Lily's own with warm fingers.

A firm—but not too firm—grip.

Hair that was a gorgeous mix of autumn. A suit that was crisp and fitted.

Eyes that were filled with intelligence and confidence.

And Lily realized why the woman was familiar.

She'd seen her on TV many times over the years.

"I'm Charlotte Harris," the other woman said. "GM of the San Francisco Gold."

THREE

WILL

He held his breath as the phone rang.

Once. Twice. Three times. Four—

Partially anyway.

"Hello?" came the breathless answer. "Will?"

He felt his lips turn up. "Yeah, Mom."

"My baby!" she exclaimed, like she did every time, like it was a surprise when he knew for a fact that his name and picture came up on the phone's screen every time he called.

Because he'd set that feature up after he'd bought her the phone.

"How are you?" he asked as he turned onto the freeway.

He was just a few minutes from the rink, so this call wouldn't be long. Which was fine—his mom was a free spirit and long phone calls weren't her thing. She needed to be unencumbered, able to flit off to the next project.

Of which there were many.

There had *always* been many.

And very few involved him.

"I'm..." His mom's voice trailed off, and he gave her a minute to refocus as he navigated the exit, turned toward the rink. He'd dubbed this the Golden Retriever Syndrome. She was easily distracted by shiny objects. And flowers. And sunshine dappling through the old glass windows of her little cottage in the woods.

Wood.

That was something else that distracted her.

The grain in planks. The bark on the living version. Leaves and pine needles and branches.

All were fascinating.

But now he was almost to the rink, and he didn't have all the time in the world to wait out her latest *Squirrel!* moment.

"Mom?" he asked, in hopes of drawing her back to reality.

Static through the speakers of his car—something else he was used to. When his mom was startled, her phone paid the price.

And his ears.

More static. More huffling.

Along with lots of fumbling.

He bit back a grin.

"Will? Honey?" she asked, voice edging toward panic. "You still there?"

The signal turned green and he accelerated. "Yeah, Mom."

"Dropped my phone," she said, still huffing.

"Yeah," he told her lightly, "I think I got that."

A pause then, "How's my baby doing?"

"I'm good, Mom. Just heading to practice."

"Oh!" she exclaimed, "I should let you go so you can get ready for it. All those pads take you a while to put on."

When he'd been a child? Absolutely.

After all these years?

"Not really," he told her. He could get dressed for the ice in about five minutes if he had to, but then again, she probably didn't spend a lot of time pondering how long it took him to get ready.

"Oh, well. I need to—"

"Mom."

Barely a moment's pause before she kept talking. "And I've got to get going myself. I need to commune with my black oak. Her leaves are looking more than a little droopy and she needs a good pep talk before winter really hits—"

"*Mom*," he said again, a little louder this time.

A beat, Golden Retriever Syndrome clearing for a minute, a hint of irritation creeping in.

She wanted to get to her tree, wanted to get back to her life. "Yeah, my baby boy?"

He buried how that made him feel, the burn of disappointment tucked deep, as he turned into the rink's parking lot. "I actually called because I needed to talk to you about the Mother-Son game."

Another beat, longer this time. "The what?"

The burn began to regenerate.

And he found he was the one who was having a moment of distraction now.

"Will?"

He focused on the somewhat sharp question. "I wanted to confirm the details about the Mother-Son game the team is putting on," he said as he pulled into a stall. "Remember, I'll fly you down here a couple of days before so we can spend some time together, and then you'll come on the team plane with the other moms when we go on the road. They have a bunch of events and fun things planned while we're busy with team stuff." Will shoved the gear shift forward, putting his car into park and pausing, waiting for her to say...something. *Anyway.* "You said you wanted to come," he finally added when she didn't. "The last time we talked I mentioned it and—"

The words stoppered up, right along with the burning humiliation. That disappointment.

He'd done this before, *felt* this before.

Too many times over the years.

"You don't have to," he found himself saying before he went any further down Memory Lane. "I'll just tell Scarlett—she's the team's publicist and is organizing the event—that you're busy. No worries at all."

Last thing he needed was her feeling guilty.

That would lead to spiraling.

Which would lead to—

Shit he didn't want to deal with.

"Oh no, no," his mom said quickly. "When is it? I-I—you know my mind slips is all. Here," she went on, like he was next to her and could see what she was doing. Then he heard paper flipping and knew she was looking at the calendar tacked to the wall in her kitchen. "Tell me when the game is?"

Throat burning, he gave her the date.

Again.

"Oh."

Christ.

He rubbed his forehead. Because he knew that tone.

"It's okay, Mom," he said. "Really. There'll be other games."

"It's just that it's my retreat weekend," she said softly, and there was regret—real regret—in her tone. Then again, there always was. "Louise and I are supposed to take this class on using cardboard and foil as collage components. It's lighter and less expensive for adding dimension, and we want to talk about it on the podcast we're starting." A laugh. "We need things to talk about it and our own lives are getting boring so we though..."

She went on.

The spiraling beginning.

Shit.

He didn't want to deal with the spiraling. Nor the meltdowns that came after.

"Mom. *Mom.*"

She stopped comparing the shiny versus the matte side of foil.

"There will be other games," he repeated. "Go to the retreat with Louise. Learn a lot so you can talk about *all* the things on your podcast."

"Really?" The childlike gasp of pleasure that paired with the question was so her.

"Really," he confirmed, ignoring the disappointment coiling in his belly. Stifling a sigh, he said, "Look, I'm at the rink—"

No sooner had he begun to speak then was she moving onto something else. "Oh! Perfect. I'll let you go, my baby! Hugs and kisses."

"By—"

The *click* hit his ears before the farewell finished crossing his lips.

Right.

There was that. Normal. Typical. His mom.

"You're lucky, man," he whispered, pocketing his cell. Lucky to have her. Lucky to have a parent who was actually in his life.

That was more than most.

He had a lot more than most in general.

A dream career. A nice house and an aggressively saved retirement fund. Friends who were like family. So, he just rode easy with his mom, took what he could get, and he'd learned long ago to let go of the things she couldn't give him, to surf the tide.

"Right," he whispered, trying to remember that fact right then. Right when the disappointment was strong and threatening to consume him. Then he popped the door and got out.

Retrieved his bag from the trunk.

Tossed it over his shoulder.

Used the familiar motions to center himself. Hockey. His job. His friends. His family. Hockey—

"You good?"

He jumped, glanced over at Brit, her blond hair swept up into a ponytail, her trademark smile not present for once.

"Yeah," he said quickly, shrugging off the call. "I was just zoning."

She'd come closer, and he watched her milk chocolate eyes narrow.

Fuck. Brit Beacon alerted.

He slapped on a smile he'd had plenty of practice donning, tucked the disappointment deep, *deep* down, and shoved Brit's shoulder. Lightly, but not too lightly because she was a professional athlete, and she was tough, and she definitely didn't want her teammates treating her with kid gloves. But also lightly because she was *his* goalie, and he wasn't going to be a dumbass and hurt her. "I stayed up too late last night playing *Call of Duty.*" He shrugged when she rolled her eyes. "Single men get to do single men things."

"Single *people* things," she corrected. "And just so you know, I'd kick your ass in *Call of Duty.*"

Never let it be said that hockey players weren't competitive.

"So says the woman who tilts her entire body when she tries to turn the camera in any video game."

Narrowed eyes on him again, but this time they were in response to his shit-giving.

Because *also* never let it be said that hockey players didn't burn each other at every opportunity.

Her chin came up, that ponytail swaying behind her head. "For the record, that helps me play better." An arch look tossed his direction. "Hence why I smoked you the last time we played."

"Well, considering *I* was playing with one hand tied behind my—"

She punched him.

Hard.

No worries about hurting *him* then.

Then again, he wasn't swiping pucks out of the air like she was and needing full functionality of his shoulders. Then again, the roster was deep and he was from the only forward in the lineup.

"Come on, asshole." She started off toward the rink then turned back and fixed him with a look he knew would scare the fuck out of any opposing player if they saw it. There was a reason she'd dominated the crease for the last decade. "Just so you know, next Board Game Night, you're going down."

Of *that*, he had no doubt.

FOUR

LILY

Charlotte Harris was standing on her porch.

Charlotte Harris, who handled annoying questions from reporters with aplomb and could rock a power suit better than anyone Lil had ever seen—man or woman—was standing on *her* porch.

In the middle of nowhere.

A tiny town close to the training facility that had been her home for the last year and a half.

Stuck in a lease in a boring, beige condo for another couple of months.

Stuck...because she didn't know what her next steps should be.

Stuck because she didn't know what—

"Can I come in?"

Lily blinked, realized she'd been standing there staring like an idiot. Staring at Charlotte Harris with her mouth gaping open and admiring her suit and—

Staring.

Oh God.

She was *still* staring.

She was going to throw up.

On Charlotte Harris's shoes. Which weren't just *shoes*. They were the nicest pair of heels she'd ever seen. A gorgeous deep gray with hints of Gold.

Gold.

Gold.

As in the *Gold* hockey team. As in, the professional hockey team. As in—

Her gaze flew up, collided with Charlotte's, who just lifted a brow.

Christ. Lil needed to get her head together. She needed—

To stop freaking *thinking* and start by inviting this woman who she admired greatly into her house.

Which was a mess.

Shit!

"I...um..." Lily swallowed and swear to God, the sound was audible, a rasping sound that echoed through the air—or maybe that was only in her ears.

She hoped so.

Or—

Enough.

Breathe. In. Two. Three. Out. Two. Three.

There.

"Please, come in," she said, glad her voice wasn't squeaky... and that she'd managed to form a complete sentence. Go her.

Charlotte hesitated.

Which made Lily realize that to actually allow the other woman to move into her condo, she needed to step *back*. She stumbled out of the opening, finally made some space for Charlotte to step over the threshold...and embarrassment cascaded over her as she turned and took in the disaster that was her life—empty takeout containers, a pizza box (also empty, because she didn't waste carbs, especially carbs that were topped with cheese), mugs and dirty cups, and paper towels.

Because she didn't bother with paper napkins.

Not when she could tuck a conveniently packaged roll under arm and get on with it.

Unfortunately, they weren't only in that convenient roll. They were also bunched up, *dirty,* sprinkled on her coffee table and couch like disturbingly large and ugly confetti.

"I'm totally addicted to this show."

Lil blinked, tore her eyes from the toxic wasteland that was her furniture, and glanced over to see that Charlotte was staring at her TV, which was paused on an unfortunate still of the villain in the middle of snarfing French fries.

"Do you think she's going to realize that he's a total scumbag?"

Lily's heart squeezed. "I hope she does before it's too late."

Charlotte's gaze drifted over. "He's charming." A tilt of her head. "Good at putting on a slick front."

He was.

Really good at it.

But now they weren't talking about the scumbag on TV.

They were talking about Zack.

"Fronts only last for so long." Lily let out a breath. "Either they get stupid and caught, or they stop caring and the front slips away."

Charlotte sucked in a breath, nodded. "I think you're right."

Lily didn't answer, mostly because she didn't know what to say.

"I want to talk about your future."

Well, that sounded ominous. "I…"

"I heard what you did."

Her heart started pounding. "With what?"

Another arched brow.

"Right." She cleared her throat, worry beginning to gather in her belly. Was this some kind of insider shake down? Like the mob? Once you cross the line in pro sports, they send a beautiful woman to exact their revenge? "Umm...well, I can't really discuss anything ongoing about... *anything.*"

"We don't need to have a discussion about *anything*," Charlotte said. "I'm not here for that."

Well, that was a relief.

No revenge by hockey skates coming her way—at least for the moment.

"Okay." She gestured to the kitchen. "Can I get you a glass of wine?"

Charlotte's expression changed—softened, warmed, and *God,* she was pretty. "Sure, Lily. I'd like that."

Lil turned for the hall, stopped when she realized that Char was following. "As a warning," she admitted, "my kitchen is an even bigger mess."

"From what I hear, your last few months have been shit."

That wasn't something she wanted to admit, but it was also the truth, so she didn't bother lying about it. "Yeah, well. They definitely haven't been the best."

"I've been there." Charlotte shrugged. "And this"—she swept out a hand—"is *nothing.* So, don't be embarrassed. I showed up without warning on your porch and interrupted your night." A smile. "And now I'm going to continue interrupting your night because I'm going to drink your wine."

Right.

Good manners aside, Lily was going to have a glass of wine with Charlotte Harris.

Eek!

She took a breath, tried to play it cool—and figured she hadn't succeeded in that in the least when Charlotte's expression did that softening and warming again. "My wine glasses are clean." A shrug. "A woman has to have her priorities."

Amusement in Charlotte's deep brown eyes. "Then we're in business."

Famous. Last. Words.

FIVE

The ball of socks hit him in the face.

This wasn't unusual.

But was he expecting it after he'd kicked ass that night?

Yeah, that was a no.

He watched it bounce off his knee, hit the floor a half second later, then searched the locker room for the culprit.

Not Josh—their captain was staring down at his phone screen, frowning.

Not Brit—who would normally be the likely shit-stirrer (and had wicked aim).

Not—

Oh. Will glared at his lineman, Lucas, who was smirking and waggling his fingers at him. "Burgers?" he asked. "Since it's a Cheat Day?"

It *was* a Cheat Day—a break from the diet plan they all followed that the team's nutritionist had put together. They got one a week, and they were heaven on Earth—mostly because Will got to eat things like burgers.

With extra cheese. And crispy bacon. And a slice of fresh tomato.

Yeah, he was a weirdo who liked a slice of tomato on his burger—weird according to Lucas, that was, who only ate fruit and vegetables because the diet plan required it. Hell, he knew the man would survive on chicken nuggies and beer if that was an option.

It wasn't.

Not when Rebecca's plan was one of the reasons they all played so damned well.

Feel good. Play good.

So Lucas gagged down his veggies.

"Sure," Will said, ripping the tape off his socks. "As long as we go to Mafia's." Which wasn't actually the name of the burger place—it was just *their* name for it, mostly because of the red velvet curtains and dark corners and black leather booths. Oh, and the pictures of old-timey mafia men on the walls and *The Godfather* looping constantly on the TVs.

And the Horse Head Burger on the menu.

"That's good with me." Lucas grinned. "Also"—a beat—"it's your turn to pay."

Damn. It *was* his turn to pay.

And Mafia's was good.

But Mafia's was expensive.

"You do realize that it's rude as fuck to make plans without including the rest of us, don't you?" Brit asked archly, now kneeling on the ground and removing her leg pads.

"As if you're going to skip beer and burgers," he tossed back. "Especially when it's my turn to pay."

A beatific smile. "I'm definitely not going to skip beer and burgers." A wink. "Especially when you're paying."

"Exactly," he muttered.

But he didn't mind.

Just like he didn't mind when some of the other guys also called out their intentions to join in. This team was his family.

The least he could do was buy a couple of beers and burgers (and fries and onion rings and potato wedges because they couldn't go to Mafia's without having the sides).

So, he focused and got undressed.

He showered.

He got *redressed*, this time in sweats and a tee and a hoodie.

Brit had already called ahead to make sure their regular table was open, so he headed to the car and was just turning on the engine when his phone rang.

Maybe it was his mom, and she'd changed her mind about—

But when he glanced at the screen, he realized it wasn't his mom. Only, for once, that didn't have disappointment coiling in his belly. Not when it was one of the two people he...well, one of the two people who weren't part of the Gold organization who'd been there for him without fail over the years.

"Don," he said, swiping across the screen and connecting the call to his car's speakers. "Hey, how are you?"

"Not good, son," was the reply.

And *that* set disappointment swirling—along with worry and no little amount of terror. Don and Valerie were good people. As were their kids, Ted and Lily. They weren't really into the hockey scene, despite Ted playing for a local recreational team, but they'd offered themselves up as a billet family when the need had arisen anyway. The Cartwrights had been the first healthy family he'd ever been around. Picket fence. Eating dinner around the table and not something microwaved into oblivion and plunked onto a tray in front of the TV. Actual conversations that included all of them—and included genuine inquiries about each other's lives. Not just the distracted, "You're not failing anything, are you, baby boy?"

Hell, Don had even made Will's lunch—sandwich, fruit, chips, and a treat—from the moment he'd begun staying there, until he'd moved onto another team.

Then they'd continued to check in, not all the time, since they were busy with their own kids, their own lives, but Don and Val both still checked in at regular intervals, and Will did the same. Not in a needy way. Just in a...they were an important part of his history way and he wanted to make sure they knew he understood that they'd given him a gift.

Stability.

Care.

Those weren't guarantees. He knew that. Viscerally.

So, bringing them out for an occasional game and catching up and Christmas gifts and the odd call here and there to connect had to be enough for Will.

He'd taken enough from them.

"What's not good?" he asked, stomach clenching.

"Lily's been going through it," Don said and sighed.

He imagined that sigh paired with Don running his hands over his face, leaving a streak of gray or blue or red paint in its wake.

Don was an artist.

He just...wasn't an artist like Will's mom.

He worked. Made money. Provided for his family—financially and emotionally.

"Have you heard about..." Don mentioned the scandal that had been on every news channel and social media platform for months.

"Um, yeah," Will said. "That's been impossible to miss. It's everywhere. Didn't the district attorney just decide to officially bring charges to the coaching staff?"

"Yes."

There was something about Don's tone that set the worry in his belly churning all over again, even more intensely than before. "It's awful what happened to those girls," Will said, "but I'm glad the case has come to light. Hopefully, those fuckers will get the book thrown at them."

"Yes."

Still, that *off* tone.

Fuck.

"Don," Will said, officially stopping beating around the bush. "What's up?"

"You can't tell anyone what I'm about to tell you."

That had the hairs on Will's nape lifting.

"Promise me that, son."

"I promise."

"No," Don said. "Really promise that this stays between us."

"When have I ever broken a promise, Don?" he asked, hurt joining that worry, especially after the phone call with his mom before practice the other day. Some people broke promises. He didn't. "This conversation stays between us, and only us."

A breath rustling through the speakers. Then Don said, "Lily was the whistleblower."

That sliced through Will like an icy blade. The person who'd illegally gathered documents and steadfastly fought against the team's management was *Lily?* "The fuck?"

"She got the job after her internship with the college team finished, and shit, Will." Don sighed. "She was so damned excited."

"It was everything she dreamed of," he said, worry eating a hole in his gut.

He spoke with Ted fairly regularly and Lily a couple of times a year, but hadn't actually seen either of the Cartwright kids since they'd moved out of their parents' house for college and graduate school—and in Lily's case—traveling all across the country chasing her dream. Ted had settled in the Midwest, was married and with a kid on the way.

Lily was...well, she was off pursuing her dream.

And that had led her into a shitstorm.

"Yeah, bud. It was her dream, and it all went bad." His voice broke slightly. "So fucking bad."

Will's hands tightened on the steering wheel. "Did he hurt her too?"

A pause that nearly had him tearing the inside of his car apart. Sweet, nice Lily, who cared about people and wanted everyone to be the best version of themselves, had found herself in a pack of wolves. "Not physically," he said. "Emotionally, though, she's had a rough go of it."

"Fuck," Will muttered.

"Wouldn't leave her kids." Don's voice was beyond rough.

"No," Will said. "She wouldn't."

"It tore her apart to stay. Especially after—" A curse. "Anyway, eventually, she got enough to blow the lid off. And she did."

She certainly had.

"Unfortunately, it landed her in a tough spot." He gave Will a rundown of the investigation that had led to Lil getting fired and the subsequent litigation.

"Why didn't you mention this to me before? I could have helped with attorney fees, at least."

"Not your responsibility, son."

Right.

Because the Cartwrights weren't his family, not really.

Even if they were in *his* heart, even *if* they occupied a space that only his teammates did.

"I would have helped."

"I know," Don said. "Which is why I know you'll help me—and Lil—now."

And then Don laid it out.

Six

She was excited.

Actually excited.

Most of her belongings were in a metal pod somewhere in the middle of the United States—and hopefully not falling off the back of the transport into a river or sitting on the trailer of an overturned big rig, burning to ash.

And hello intrusive thoughts, thank you for visiting. Now go bye-bye.

Rolling her eyes internally, she tugged her backpack from beneath the seat in front of her and clutched it to her chest, shuffling out with the rest of the cattle to make her way up the aisle of the plane.

San Francisco.

She'd made it.

A fresh start...*and* she was going to see Will.

God, it had been years but her heart still gave a little pitter-patter just thinking his name.

Will.

Teenage heartthrob.

Flow for *days*.

More muscles than any boy her age.

Because he was four years older than her, supremely talented, and...totally saw her as nothing more than an annoying twelve-year-old little sister.

Which was a good thing—it was the *right* thing. The *only* thing.

He'd been sixteen. On a whole other planet. Mature in ways her middle school crush did *not* allow for, didn't understand. *Couldn't* understand because of the years between them.

But—God—she'd loved him in a way that had been *intense*.

And he'd only reciprocated with brotherly affection.

Crushing.

Yet the only way it could be.

And now she was moving in with him, working on the same team he played for.

That hadn't processed—not for long after Charlotte Harris had left the job offer on her kitchen counter, sandwiched between a roll of paper towels and their two empty wineglasses.

"I heard what you did," Charlotte had said. "And I can think of no one better to have on the payroll."

Lily's heart still rolled over in her chest at the memory.

At the respect in Charlotte's voice—not begrudging, but bright and out there and so obviously expressed. From one of her heroes. Respect for her actions and her choices and—

There had never been a moment Lil hadn't considered taking the job.

Working under Charlotte Harris.

Working with a professional—*professional!*—sports team.

Putting together a program under the umbrella of player development because they had nothing in place and Char—yup, *Charlotte Harris* wanted Lily to call her *Char*—wanted Lily to put a program to protect the mental health of her players together.

Protect her players.

Not a commodity, but people with real feelings and emotions.

God, that had filled her heart with *joy*.

So much so that she'd called her parents, not registering it was after midnight, that she and Charlotte had spent hours talking about the team and Char's plans going forward, all while finishing two bottles of wine, not registering at first that the man who'd quietly knocked on the door to remind Char of their flight was Logan, a Gold player with a beard that screamed lumbersexual and dark green eyes that were the color of ancient forests.

That had only hit after he'd bundled Char into their car and driven off and Lil had returned to the kitchen, the folder with the Gold logo on the counter—

And recognized it had been real.

So then had called her parents.

Her mom had picked up.

Of course she had.

She always did, but also, Lil knew her parents had been on high alert since everything had gone down. An after-midnight phone call in the middle of the week probably hadn't inspired a whole lot of reassurance.

But her mom had grabbed her dad, and she'd told them about the offer—

And now she was here.

In San Francisco.

And...staying with Will, courtesy of her dad. Something she normally wouldn't be okay with, except that Will had insisted, despite her speaking with him earlier in the week, intending to let him off the hook from her dad's demands.

"You're coming to San Francisco and working with my team, Lil," he'd said. *"Don't even try to get out of staying with me. We're family. We take each other's backs."*

Her heart went pitter-patter again.

Will taking *her* back. Her staying with him. Family. *Aw.*

She commanded the organ to relax. They'd kept in touch over the years and he was just thankful for the year he'd lived with her family. That was all. This was a favor to her parents and nothing more. Plus, he was a good guy, and she was going to work for the team. It was just a nice offer from a nice guy for a place to stay until the apartment she'd leased became available.

Big house.

Plenty of bedrooms.

He'll look out for you.

That from her dad less than a day after she'd given her parents the good news.

And maybe she should be offended that he'd bypassed her and arranged things with Will, that Will had accepted without talking to her, without even seeing her...but it came from a place of care, *and* it had gotten her out of her condo when things had been moving in warp speed. From the moment that Charlotte Harris had turned up on her porch to the job offer. Her accepting it. Moving to San Francisco.

All in a week.

Because the season had started and there was work to be done and she was already behind where she should be if she'd been on the payroll since the beginning—

Someone bumped her from behind and she realized she'd stopped in the middle of the pathway, still clutching her backpack and zoning out as she stared up at the monitors looking for the number of her bag claim. Right. She was in San Francisco. She was about to start her new job.

That required focus.

No more zoning. Eyes forward and locked on her fresh start. To go backward was...

Not something she could allow herself.

She noted the baggage claim number then started forward, hitching her backpack over her shoulders.

Then she rode the escalator down, gaze scanning.

And *finding*.

Her heart did that pitter-patter again.

Will was...God. He was *huge,* head and shoulders over the

people waiting with him, over those milling around behind him. Eyes that were a piercing blue—she'd written *that* in a long-ago diary entry.

Grinning, she hurried over to him, backpack bouncing with each stride.

She'd checked two bags, but her life was in her backpack.

Hence the previous clutching.

Lily opened her mouth as she got within arm's length of Will. His beard had hints of red in it, and there was a tattoo creeping up the left side of his neck, slender black tendrils of ink that had her wanting to tug down the collar of his shirt.

Just for curiosity's sake.

Not because he was looking like a snack she wanted to pound and—

Right.

Pounding.

Probably not the best thing to be thinking about her former crush and the man who was doing her a favor now.

She was close enough to scent his cologne, and yeah, that was yummy too.

It made her nose tingle. It made other parts tingle too. It—

"I'm not interested."

She blinked at the rough rumble, and it took her a minute to realize it had come from Will. Mostly because his tone was deep and different from when he'd been a kid, from when they spoke on the phone, but also because it was different because...it held no warmth.

Just ice and frost.

"Will."

"Like I said"—a disdainful glance in her direction—"I'm *not* interested."

Lily felt her nostrils flare in annoyance. Yes, she was ogling. Yes, he was hot.

But seriously? Ego much?

Apparently, more had changed in the last decade than she'd expected.

"Cute, Will," she said dryly. "But I figured I should at least say hi to the man whose house I'm staying in before I get my luggage."

His face changed, scowl dropping away, shock in his eyes as they dropped to her feet and then slid back up. "Lil?"

And hell, if she didn't feel that tracing gaze deep in her belly.

Trouble.

Trouble. Trouble. Trouble.

Why did she hear Ray LaMontagne's voice when she thought that?

"Yup," she said, lifting her chin. "That's still my name." Then —heart still pitter-pattering—she flounced off toward the baggage claim. Well, flounced as much as she was able to with her backpack containing her life's most important belongings weighing down her shoulders, but she supposed she managed to flounce enough because she barely made it ten feet away before big, warm fingers were wrapping around her arm, hauling her to a stop. "Lily," he said. "I'm sorry. I—"

She forced a smile, turned toward him, and knew she needed to extend an olive branch if she wanted to make this marginally less awkward. "Hey," she said. "It's good. It's been a while." Her smile widened, and she knew she probably looked like a lunatic.

It was just...

The utter surprise got her.

Like there hadn't been one moment of thought given to the fact that she'd grown up in the years that had passed, that she wasn't a child any longer...and his shock made her feel like she was twelve again.

Simpering after a man who wanted nothing to do with her and—

Down that thought went, shoved into the box, the lid slammed down and locked.

"We're not teenagers anymore," she said, forcing her tone to be light. She patted his fingers where they'd wrapped around her arm. "We're all grown up now." A wave of her hand down her body. "*I'm* all grown up."

A grunt as he jerked away, as though her touch was anathema—

She cut *that* thought off too, and down into the box it went.

"I—" she began.

He turned away. "Let's go get your bags."

She watched the long, strong lines of his body ripple as he walked.

And didn't look back.

And...right.

Lil sighed and trailed after him.

This couldn't possibly be going worse.

SEVEN

Will

Fuck. Fuck. *Fuck.*

He glanced down at his dick, at the traitorous organ that was being a real asshole in his pants—and sent mental orders to cool it.

This was Lily.

Lily.

The girl with frizzy blond hair and braces was...a woman.

All grown up as she'd said.

Except it was that she was all grown. *Everywhere.* She had breasts and hips and when she turned and bent to grab a heavy bag off the carousel—something *he* should be getting for *her*—his cock was definitely not behaving.

Not cooling it.

Not helpful.

Especially when he needed to get past his shock and not be a total douchebag, to help her as she struggled to lift her bag off the rotating silver platform. Be chivalrous...except he couldn't.

Because he was hard.

Fuck.

Her bending and lifting that bag wasn't helping his situation.

Things were jiggling and flexing and—

The hem of her fluffy blue sweater lifted, giving him a glimpse of ink at the base of her spine—and fuck him senseless, Lily, little Lily Cartwright with the frizzy blond hair and braces and glasses that always slid down her nose, who'd stared after him like he held the keys to the universe, had a goddamned tramp stamp.

His cock continued misbehaving.

His *cock* wanted her bent over, that tattoo on display as he fucked her from behind.

His cock *needed* to be glistening with evidence of her desire as he pulled out of her wet pussy and finished on that ink.

His cock—

"Christ," he muttered, reaching past her, bumping into her as he extended his hand and yanked at the bag, hefting the purple floral-patterned suitcase off the baggage carousel and setting it onto the floor with a thump. "Sorry," he said, still muttering, grabbing her arm and steadying her since he was a big asshole who was apparently trying to check a woman he was supposed to be looking after to the dirty airport tiles.

And hey now, *that* wasn't the only thing dirty, if Lily's tramp stamp was any indication.

"Fuck," he gritted out, his dick pressing against his zipper.

"Most of my life is in a storage container and I don't know when it'll be here," she said softly, hurt in her words. Wrongly assuming he was grumbling about grabbing her bag off the carousel. "I had to bring enough to get me started."

Great.

Now he was an asshole who was cursing at her and trying to check her to the floor and making her feel bad *and* creeping on a girl who...

Was a woman.

Who was looking at him with hurt in her eyes.

And Christ, Don had asked him to look after Lily and he was...

Getting hard-ons and yelling at her.

After she'd had a shitty few years. Hell, after she'd had more than that. Her dream shattered. A horrible work situation. Legal troubles and...starting over.

"Lil," he said quietly.

Her body was turned from his, that sweater safely covering the tattoo, thank fuck. Although the hem was teasing the middle of her ass which was definitely *not* something he wanted to be noticing. Or should be.

Or—

Her shoulders were hitched up, arms wrapped around her middle, the fingertips just visible on the sides of that backpack.

Which looked heavy.

Fuck.

He moved closer. "Lil," he murmured, grabbing the handle at the top, sliding it down her arms. He hooked it on top of the giant ass suitcase, and tugged her back, positioned the bags next to her. "Point out the rest of your stuff."

Her gaze was glued to the carousel. "It's just one more bag."

Soft.

Hurt.

Fuck.

Will tugged lightly at the end of her ponytail. "I'm sorry."

She didn't look at him.

"I'm also an asshole who was in a shit mood," he said, "thinking that someone was bothering me when I was looking forward to seeing an old friend."

Her shoulders hitched up further. "That happen a lot?"

It...

Didn't *not* happen a lot.

Now she glanced up at him, and her face had softened. "It happens a lot."

He shrugged. He wasn't a player by any means, but he didn't have trouble getting women, especially in the hockey crazy Bay

Area. A successful team meant getting recognized, meant... women.

But his life had been filled with impermanence.

He craved...connection, not hookups.

Getting off was empty and left him alone on important dates and feeling like a fucking sleaze ball.

He blamed all the happy fuckers on the team.

The little family units that made up the Gold. He'd seen too many happy marriages and kids being born and team events with everyone hanging out peacefully to not want what they had.

Will just wasn't convinced the same future would be in the cards for him.

"So," she murmured, bumping her shoulder against his, jogging him back into the present, and reminding him of that big generous heart of hers. "Should we just chalk this up to the worst roomie reunion ever and start over?"

Relief slid through him, managing to get even his misbehaving cock to take a note and chill the fuck out.

Because starting over sounded perfect.

He'd bleach his thoughts, shove Lily firmly back into the little sister category.

"Depends," he said.

Wariness in pretty hazel eyes. "On what?"

"Can you still snipe like a rockstar?"

"*Halo* or *Call of Duty?*"

He lifted a brow. "What do you think?"

"Both," she said, mouth curving up at the edges. "But mostly *Call of Duty* if my memory serves correctly. Not that it matters" —she buffed her knuckles on her shoulder—"I still kick ass at both."

Little Sister Mode activated.

"That's right, baby." He lifted a fist, waited till she bumped it. "I knew I could count on you."

Her lips curved.

"Lil?"

She sobered, probably because any humor had left his tone. "Yeah?"

"I'd really like to start over," he said softly. "If it's cool with you."

Her mouth hitched up again, relief in the browns and golds of her eyes. "Good," she said then tilted her head toward the carousel. "Because that's my second bag, and I almost broke my back trying to get the first one off there."

He took the hint and, grinning, he reached beyond her to haul the bag off, rolling it toward the other. "Anything else?"

He'd meant bags.

But she either didn't get that or didn't care. "I'm hungry."

"Then I think it's time to feed you." Amusement coiled in his belly. Because that hadn't changed. The girl he'd known all those years ago had always been hungry. He tugged her ponytail again, laughing when she swatted lightly at him. Then he grabbed the handles of both suitcases before she could and asked, "What do you like?"

Her stomach rumbled. "Anything, but I wouldn't turn down a giant bowl of fries."

"Burgers?"

Her stomach rumbled again.

He grinned. "I know a place."

———

Thankfully, he managed to feed her without being an asshole.

Mostly because he'd fed her, thus had spent a good portion of the meal with his mouth full.

Meaning, they didn't speak much.

And now he was dragging her heavy ass bags up the stairs and thinking their conditioning coach, Jen, would very much approve of the workout he was getting.

His quads...yup, they were burning.

And glutes and hammies and biceps and—

"Will?"

He looked up, realized he was holding her bags and standing in the doorway of the guest bedroom. Zoning out. With his entire body burning. *Right.* So slick and cool and not awkward at all. Also...this would be the time to drop the bags then give her some space. A slight internal shake of his head as he brought the suitcases in and dropped them in the empty closet, telling her to "Settle in however makes you the most comfortable."

Her eyes danced with mirth. "Most comfortable?"

God, he sounded like a fucking idiot.

He cleared his throat. "Yeah."

A tilt of her head. "Does this comfort involve me making midnight trips to your pantry for Double Stuf Oreos?"

His mouth tipped up and he managed to act like a normal person for approximately two seconds to tease, "Why do you think I bought three packs?"

Soft eyes now. *Dangerous* eyes...for his dick. "Thanks," she whispered.

Then yawned.

"Sleep time, Lil," he murmured, stepping toward the door before he did something stupid like brush that strand of hair out of her face and tuck it behind her ear.

Before he told her it was kind of nice to have someone else in his house.

Told her it made him feel less alone.

Told her—

She yawned again, dragging her fingers over her cheek and roughly shoving the hair off her face.

Focus.

"Bathroom's through the other door," he told her. "And the kitchen is stocked, but let me know if you need anything I forgot, and I'll pick it up."

"I'm sure I'll be fine." That strand escaped once more, and she pushed it back again. "Thanks for picking me up from the airport." Her eyes drooped, but her smile was gentle. "And for schlepping my bags up the stairs." Another yawn. Another smile. "And for dinner."

God, she was pretty. "Anytime, Lil."

"And"—she fought that piece of hair again, blowing out an exasperated sigh—"for letting me stay."

He gave in, leaning close and tucking that strand behind her ear, making sure it wouldn't escape again.

At least for a few seconds.

"Anytime, Lil," he said again.

Her lips were parted, eyes tired, skin like silk.

"Night," she whispered.

He blinked.

Then he got his ass out of that room before he did something even more stupid.

Eight

She sighed as she stood under the stream of hot water, letting it run over her body.

The water pressure was chef's kiss.

As was the fact that the man had a tankless water heater, so the hot gloriousness of a long shower never turned cold.

It had been a week since she had taken up residence in Will's house...and it had been surprisingly calm and quiet and absent of the awkwardness from the airport.

Mostly because the season was in full swing and he'd been at the rink more than his house.

Something that felt familiar to Lil.

He'd spent a lot of time at the rink during that year he'd lived with her family—at practice, training off the ice or putting in his time in the weight room, traveling to games. That was no different now, especially considering that this was now his job, and he took it seriously, so his commitment was even more encompassing.

All of which meant she'd pretty much had his place to herself as she unpacked her heavy suitcases and stalked the location of her belongings that were scheduled to arrive in the next couple of weeks and took way longer than anticipated recovering from her jet lag.

It was only a couple of time zones, but sweet baby Jesus, she didn't know how Will made it through an entire season of these changes.

Hockey skills.

Jet lag superpowers.

Anyway, she'd grabbed a quick lunch with Char to get the lay of the land at the practice facility and confirm some of their plans —since the GM was busy with her day-to-day duties. Then Lil had spent time putting together the basics of what she wanted her program to look like.

And today—eek—she was going in to fill out her official paperwork.

Today she would become a real part of the Gold family.

She couldn't wait.

Just thinking of the laughter and ease of the interactions she'd witnessed during her tour of the facility between Charlotte and the rest of the staff, the players, hearing the teasing and inside jokes, had a sense of *rightness* settling in her belly.

She now knew how important that was.

The hallways outside Zack's office had been silent.

Lily had thought that accounted for seriousness, credibility.

She knew differently now.

Thank God.

Exhaling, she forced herself to push the handle in, to shut off the stream of water, and then reached for the towel she'd hung over the top of the glass door...only she didn't feel the fluffy end of the white cotton sheet.

Swiping a finger over her lashes, she squinted, saw it wasn't there.

It. Wasn't. There.

Why wasn't it there?

"Because you didn't put it there, dummy," she muttered, glancing around the room like it would magically appear—or that her robe, currently in the washer, would just poof onto the hook outside the large glass door.

Spoiler alert, it didn't.

"Crap," she whispered, squeezing out the ends of her hair so they weren't dripping cold, wet water down her spine.

Then she pushed the door open, braced against the cool air, and stepped out onto the rug.

Bent and looked in the cabinet beneath the sink.

Empty.

Well, there was a roll of toilet paper and an ancient-looking bottle of bathroom cleaner, but the remainder of the cabinet was empty of towels.

And she'd just thrown the ones she'd been using into the washer along with her robe.

And...it was cold.

"Shit," she muttered, shifting from foot to foot, dripping onto the bathmat, debating what to do.

Laundry room? That would involve her walking naked through the house.

Linen closet? That was almost as bad. It was in full view of the front door, and with her luck, she'd flash the Amazon guy.

Will's bathroom was just across the hall. She could—

"No," she whispered, yanking the hand towel off the ring, wiping her body...and making absolutely no progress in drying her body off.

Okay, so it was a *little* progress—as in, it was *really* little.

And she was cold and wet and *still* dripping on the mat.

Right. She needed to stop being cold and wet and do something about it.

Will was at practice, and he would be there for a little while yet. She could just zip through his bedroom, snag a towel from his en suite, and be on her way. In no time, she would be snug and cozy in a towel that would cover more than one of her breasts.

Cool.

Good plan.

The *only* plan.

Wrapping the tiny tea towel around the ends of her hair—because the cold beads they were dropping on her skin weren't her friends—she hustled out of the bathroom, through the guest room that had become hers, and darted across the hall.

The knob turned under her hand.

The door slid open.

And yes, she was dissociating between her actions and her body because this was really wrong, invading Will's space, his privacy, and she shouldn't be doing it, and—

Her toes hit the plush pile of the area rug positioned beneath his bed, and she paused.

That was a really big bed.

It was unmade, with crisp white sheets and a pale blue duvet, the pattern faint enough that she found herself squinting and leaning closer, getting a hint of his aftershave as she deduced it was a fine plaid.

Her hand moved, this time of its own volition, reaching for the edge of the covers, wanting to straighten it, to make the bed, to put everything in its proper place. Thankfully, reason returned when her fingers touched the soft cotton, and she jerked back, forced herself to focus.

"Towel," she whispered. "Get a damned towel and get out."

Right. Good plan.

She hurried into the bathroom, stunned into stillness again.

Because this bathroom was *lush.*

It was exquisite.

Double sinks sunk into a cream vanity, the top a faint blue that echoed the duvet. Plenty of counter space, a built-in vanity, lights that would aid in putting makeup on instead of making her look like a vampire.

The tub was...huge.

Big enough to fit Will and a lady friend.

Hell, maybe even three lady friends.

A bolt of jealousy in her belly, but that was a familiar feeling —albeit one she hadn't suffered for approximately a decade.

The shower had...*three* shower heads. And a hand shower. And a little seat on one end.

It would be perfect for her to rest one foot on while she shaved her legs.

A partially closed door hid most of the toilet.

Another revealed a huge closet that was—and she peeked... because of course she peeked—only a quarter full.

Gorgeous.

Every piece of trim. Every shelf. Every faucet and hinge and tile.

The whole place was the most beautiful bathroom she'd ever stepped foot in.

Only...it felt half-finished, half-empty.

As though it was waiting for something.

Or someone.

Was Will waiting for someone?

That was almost enough for her to forget about being cold, to focus on what she knew about Will. She'd been careful to tuck it all away, to not focus on it. A crush bordering on obsession might have been cute as a twelve-year-old, but it was inversely proportional to increasing age.

And she was an adult woman.

Obsession definitely wasn't cute now.

Especially since she was staying in his house. Standing in his gorgeous bathroom. Wondering why a man as sexy and nice as Will was still single.

So not the time.

"Towel," she ordered herself, marching forward toward the closed door between the closet and toilet that she assumed was hiding the linen closet, and reached for the handle.

A slam had her jumping and turning around.

Then gasping and clinging to the washcloth.

"Will!"

NINE

WILL

Wet.

Frowning, he glanced down, saw—and well, *felt*—the wet carpet beneath his feet.

"Fuck," he muttered.

The plumber was supposed to have fixed that pipe in his bathroom. If he'd come home again and it was leaking, swear to fucking *God*—

Tossing his jacket on the bed, he stormed forward, yanking off his shirt, dropping it to his feet, vaguely noting the dampness and mentally sending the plumber to the seventh circle of hell.

It had cost him ten grand and had been a huge pain in the ass to redo his fucking bathroom after the pipes had burst the first time.

If the same damned thing had happened again...

He'd create a whole damned *new* circle of hell.

"Christ," he muttered, flicking open the button on his slacks, tugging down the zipper, stepping out of them. He knew how this worked. He'd be mopping up the floor for the rest of the night to clean up this fucking shit. And use every damned towel in the process.

Cursing under his breath, he shoved open the bathroom door—

For a second, he didn't understand what he was seeing.

He even deliberately blinked because it wasn't a leak. It was—

Holy fucking shit.

But then the door he'd pushed open hit the wall and the woman in front of him gasped and spun around. No. *Lily* gasped and spun to face him, a tiny towel clutched to her front that did absolutely nothing to conceal lush breasts and—

Fuck. She was a natural blond.

Of course she was a natural blond.

He'd known that. He'd seen her when she was a child.

A child.

Christ. Fuck. Shit. *Fuck.*

He started to back out of the room.

"Will!" she gasped.

Her breasts jiggled, nipples in hard, rosy points that called for his mouth. His fingers. His teeth and tongue and—

She had a freckle just beneath her belly button, like a stopping point for his lips before he got his mouth between her legs.

"I-I'm sorry," she whispered. "I didn't have any towels, and I thought you were still at practice."

More jiggling, but worse this time.

Because he'd stopped backing out of the room.

Because she'd crossed her arm over her breasts, plumping them, all while that towel slid southward, covering her belly button, her freckle, the small patch of curls that concealed a pussy his mouth was suddenly watering for—

He slammed his eyes closed.

Not mouthwatering.

Not having the gorgeous image of Lily and all of her curves burned on his retina.

Not having to clench his hands into fists so he didn't close the distance between them and show her exactly how much he wanted to make a pit stop on that freckle before picking her up, plunking her onto the counter, and getting his mouth between her thighs.

Not—

"Will," she whispered.

His eyes flew open.

Hers went wide, nostrils flaring on an inhale.

"Lil," he growled.

"Don't look at me like that," she whispered.

He took a step forward. "Like what?"

Her throat worked. "Like you—" She broke off, shook her head.

"Like what?" he asked again.

Lips parting, plump and kissable. A shaky breath that drew his focus back to her breasts.

He took another step forward and now he was close enough to see she had another freckle, this one on her collarbone.

"Will," she whispered.

His gaze drifted back to hers, and the heat in her eyes...

Fuck it.

He reached for her, fingers brushing her arms, and hell if her skin wasn't like silk. He drew her closer, not stopping until their bodies were touching.

Bare skin against bare skin.

She gasped again, arm dropping so that her breasts were pressed to his chest, and what he wouldn't give to taste that little puff of air on his tongue, to feel it drift across his cock. What he wouldn't give to taste every single inch of her.

"Will," she whispered, leaning more heavily against him.

He bent, inhaling deeply—sweet and woman and *need* filling every cell in his body. His lips brushed that silken skin on her cheek, her throat—

And her dad's voice echoed through his mind.

Which is why I know you'll help me—and Lil—now.

Help Lily.

By taking advantage of her?

Another feminine sigh, her body leaning more heavily against his, tempting him, making him want what he couldn't have. He felt it in his cock, but not just there. He felt it everywhere, felt it deeply, almost deeply enough to forget that voice, to forget what he'd promised her dad.

Her dad.

Who'd been more of a father than his own piece of shit sperm donor.

Who'd done more for him, and Will was—

Fuck. *Fuck.*

He jerked back, so quickly Lily started to topple forward and all the distance between them disappeared as she fell against him, the tiny towel falling to the floor, all of her naked body pressed to his almost naked one. Curves. Soft. Woman. *His.*

To protect.

Not to grope in the bathroom.

He jerked again, more carefully this time, making sure she was steady this time.

"I—" she whispered, lifting her hand.

If she touched him again, he'd lose it. That last little bit of control he'd managed to cobble together would poof out of existence.

And he'd—

"Don't fucking touch me," he snapped, putting more distance between him.

Her face.

Fuck, it killed him.

But he couldn't do this.

He reached past her, yanked a towel off the rack and tossed it at her. Thank fuck, she caught it and the cotton sheet unrolled, covering her almost to her toes, erasing the temptation of her—

Fuck.

Who was he kidding?

She *was* temptation.

"You're not twelve anymore and I'm not sixteen," he growled, hands in fists at his sides. "I'm just doing you a fucking favor by letting you stay here and that's all this is." A breath, trying to moderate his tone. "Don't forget that."

He expected her to crumple—that expression on her face was pure hurt. But instead, she just lifted her chin, looking like a fucking goddess as she clutched that towel to her front.

"Are you worried that I forgot?" she asked, voice ice-*fucking*-cold. "Or that you did?"

He didn't have an answer to that—or maybe he didn't *want* to answer it.

Not that it mattered.

She brushed by him, and he forced himself to not turn, to not allow himself another glimpse of that ass.

Only when he heard the door to the guest room shut—not slam, because Lil wouldn't slam the door, wouldn't stoop that low—did he grab his pants, his shirt from his bedroom, and practically tear them trying to get them on.

Feet into shoes.

Ass in his car.

He drove away, stayed the fuck away until he was sure she would be asleep.

Only when he came home, the guest room door was open, and the light was on.

"Fuck," he muttered, knowing he owed her more than an apology, knowing he needed to smooth this over, knowing he needed find a way to pretend the scene in the bathroom hadn't happened even though every time he closed his eyes he saw her naked, even though his fingertips still tingled from the feel of her skin beneath them.

But when he moved into the open doorway, his gut twisted.

The regret that had burned through him for hours ramped again, eviscerating him from the inside out.

Because the guest room was empty.

Ten

Lily

Her hands shook as she approached the arena a few days later.

Will had called and texted, but he hadn't tracked her down. Probably because he'd had to leave the morning after Bathroom Gate for an away game.

So she hadn't replied to his texts, had used the time to sort out her shit.

She knew it was immature, that it was likely in her best interest to smooth over what had happened in his bathroom. His outburst was...surprise. That was it. Well, that and whatever twisted emotions had made heat and guilt write themselves into the lines of his face, the blue of his eyes.

He wanted to see her as a little sister.

And she'd been naked in his bathroom, *not* looking like a little sister.

So...heat, which—she couldn't lie—had felt good. The little girl who'd crushed on him liked the heat, that he might see her as something more than a child. What hadn't? The guilt on his face —like he was doing something awful and wrong by being attracted to her, even though they were both grown adults who could make their own decisions now.

She exhaled.

The guilt was why she'd packed her stuff and gone. She didn't like the way it made her feel and she didn't want to be the cause of whatever twisted emotions were eating him alive. If she stayed... there would be more conflict, more guilt.

So...she'd gotten a hotel.

Something that was the easy way out.

Avoidance. Not actually dealing with the issues, with the guilt. Not dealing with the conflict and how yucky that guilt on his face had made her feel, how the sharp, accusatory tone he'd used when he pulled back had left her sliced to ribbons.

Luckily, San Francisco had plenty of hotels.

Luckily, an apartment opened up earlier than expected where she'd planned on living. The bonus was that it was on the top floor and in the corner with a nice view of the trees surrounding the complex.

Was it more expensive than she'd wanted?

Sure was.

Was it exactly what she needed to get the hell away from whatever toxic bullshit was brewing between her and Will so they could go back to being friends and co-workers?

Yup.

Was she delaying, clinging to the metal bar that would let her into the building?

Abso-fucking-lutely.

"You don't actually *have* to go in there, you know?"

Lil blinked and glanced over her shoulder at the tall blond coming her way.

And recognized her instantly.

Brit Plantain.

Resident badass and the first female player in the league—the *only* female player in the league. Lily hadn't met her yet, had actually expected her to be in the locker room with the rest of the team getting ready for their game. There was a reason she was coming in for her first day at the arena now—and that was avoidance of a certain brown-haired, blue-eyed man who looked at her like he wanted to both fuck her and shove her into a closet (alone) and slam the door shut (with them on opposite sides of it)—

Brit moved closer and Lily snapped out of it.

"Sorry," she said, sticking her hand out. "I was thinking of my very long mental to-do list." *Liar.* "I'm Lily."

"I know," Brit replied with a smile that had graced many an advertisement. "I'm Brit."

"I know," Lil quipped, which earned her a chuckle. "It's nice to meet you."

"Likewise." Brit tilted her head toward the door. "Want to do the honors? Or should I?"

Lily sucked in a breath, released it silently. "I've got it," she said and pulled open the door, holding it so Brit could walk through. "That way you can save your strength for stopping all those shots on the ice."

Brit grinned. "Meh, the guys will block them for me."

Lil chuckled.

"Plus, I already did my warmup. I just needed to pop home to give goodnight cuddles."

"Your little one?" Lily asked, heart melting at the way Brit's face had gentled.

"She's the best." Brit grinned, snagging her phone and showing Lily a picture of an adorable little girl. "Though I also find the hubs needs just as many goodnight cuddles."

Lily giggled. "I imagine that's the case."

Brit smiled then tilted her head down the hall. "Need a tour guide to your office?"

The question wasn't irritated or annoyed or impatient—even though Lily had been standing like a lump, blocking Brit's ability to get inside the rink. It was a genuine offer. And, God, Brit was nice. Lil had heard that through the grapevine. But to see evidence that it was real, that it wasn't an act, that she had further proof being *here* was right, felt...like a warm fluffy blanket settled around her shoulders.

She wanted to stay wrapped in it forever.

Still, Lil shook her head. "I should let you get on the ice."

Brit grinned. "Yeah, I guess I should do that thing called playing hockey." She started to walk away, paused and turned back. "Hey, are you going to join us for the team dinner on Saturday?"

That was definitely not avoidance of a certain blue-eyed hockey player. "I..."

"We're family here," Brit said softly, reaching out and squeezing Lily's arm. "And that means everyone is included."

A breath. Pushing the urge to avoid away.

"I'll be there."

Brit smiled. "Good." Then she was off down the hall and Lil didn't miss that she tapped the Gold logo on the wall—presumably in a pregame ritual—before she disappeared around the corner.

Presumably because all athletes were superstitious.

Presumably because Lil knew that hockey players were especially so—needing to wear a certain pair of socks or a helmet that was old or a special shirt or the way they taped their stick or even getting dressed in a certain order. Tapping doorframes. *Logos.* Being the first or last on the ice or in the locker room.

They all had their little things.

Brit would certainly be no different.

Though now it seemed her pregame had evolved to include cuddles—something that left Lily with a smile on her face as she headed to her office.

To work.

To focus.

To make the most of this opportunity.

No more thoughts of Will, of the scene in the bathroom, of the guilt and the sharp words and how all of that had made her feel.

She didn't think about the dozen towels she'd ordered off Amazon, so she would never run out of them again.

She just focused on why she was here.

On work.

On the one thing that was safe.

The *one* thing that had never let her down.

———

She'd mistimed.

She'd ended up watching the game from the team's box over-head, eyes glued to the ice, breath catching at the speed and size and strength of the men—and woman—below. Lily had already memorized the players' numbers and names, but she hadn't gotten there on stats yet. It was a lot of data to cross reference, so she spent plenty of time glancing from the rink to her roster and make notes of who was playing and how they were playing and then cross-referencing that with how their stats were progressing.

That was one useful thing about starting a job like this with the season already under way.

There was already data to crunch, and the players were already firmly in their routines.

So now she just needed to tweak them.

Which was why she'd had a smile on her face, her mind going a million miles a minute, full of plans, excitement in every inch of her body, as she stepped out of her office.

And nearly ran smack dab into a certain sexy, blue-eyed hockey player.

She sucked in a breath, pulse pounding in her veins, heat coiling between her legs—because holy fucking shit, the man was a goddamned *God*, and the last time she'd been this close to him she'd been naked and he was shirtless and—

He was sweaty. Now. Not then.

Something that should be disgusting.

Instead, it threatened to melt her into a puddle.

Because his hair had gone slightly curly and his skin glistened and he was *huge*, still in his skates, those pads caressing each and every one of the hard lines of his body she'd felt pressed to her body.

Hot.

So fucking hot that she could pretend the guilt hadn't existed and—

"Where the fuck have you been?" he snapped.

Okay, that wasn't hot.

Definitely *not* hot.

Her eyes narrowed, and in a second, he became a big, tall, good-looking (unfortunately) asshole. She called up all of her training, breathed for a count of four in and then four out. "Hi, Will," she chirped. "Nice game tonight."

He snorted, disregarding her lie. He'd been one of the guys struggling that night. "Sure." He stepped closer—and fuck her dumbass self, but he smelled delicious. Salty and spicy and how in the hell did he smell delicious after working his ass off for the last three hours?

It made no sense.

He bent so his face was close to hers, blue eyes flashing. "You haven't picked up any of my calls, haven't sent a fucking text. If I hadn't talked to your parents, I wouldn't have known you were okay."

Her nostrils flared, annoyance in her belly. "I'm a grown woman, Will. I don't need you to check up on me."

A hand thumping to his chest. "I'm responsible for you—"

Now she was the one who snorted. "No," she said flatly. "I'm still a grown ass woman. You don't need to check up on me with my fucking parents—" He moved even closer and her voice stoppered up, words sticking in the back of her throat.

Close and big and strong and—

His words were hot. "I'm not going to let you—"

Let you.

No.

Yeah. That snapped her out of it, thankfully. Because just...*no.*

She glared and rose up on tiptoe, barely resisting the urge to jab him in the chest. "You're not going to *let* me do anything," she snapped. "I'm going to live my life and do my job, and you're going to do the same, and if—and when—our lives overlap, we'll deal." She didn't resist the jab this time, not that he probably felt it through those pads. "And we'll deal with it like fucking adults." She sucked in a breath, released it, and dropped back onto her heels. "I already apologized...for the bathroom," she forced herself to say calmly. "But again, I'm sorry that happened."

His expression sobered, gentleness entering his eyes.

Also, just...*no.*

She narrowed her eyes, steeled her spine. "So can we forget it and start over and just get the fuck on with the rest of our lives?"

More gentle.

More warm.

Maybe a dash of heat from him remembering—and yeah, she couldn't go *that* way.

So, she *went* away.

Didn't wait for him to answer, just hustled back into her office and shut the door firmly, flicking the lock for good measure.

Getting the hell on with the rest of her life.

Without Will fucking it up.

Eleven

He'd tried to slide into the locker room like he hadn't just fought with the woman whose life he was supposed to be making easier.

Unfortunately, sneaking wasn't one of his great life skills.

A decent wrist shot, good hands, and will—no pun intended—to chase down any puck. *Those* were in his wheelhouse.

Sneaking. Brooding. Escaping the notice of a certain goalie who'd made it her life's mission to keep her little hockey ducklings in a row?

Not so much.

Brit was sitting next to him, having squeezed herself right between him and Lucas, even though space was at a premium, considering that Lucas was a big motherfucker.

So needless to say, Brit was close.

Close enough to study every facet of his expression.

And seriously, who in the fuck needed a Lily when they had a Brit in the locker room?

A Brit who was retiring at the end of this season—something that sent a pang through Will's heart. They would miss her.

A whole fucking lot.

Except...during conversations like this.

Her milk chocolate eyes fixed him in place.

"You've been off lately," she said quietly.

Yeah, ever since he'd punched his asshole card.

What might work for other guys was Will's kryptonite. He hated that he'd hurt Lily, hated that his attraction to her felt wrong and yet so fucking *right* he couldn't stop thinking about her. But most of all, he hated that she'd left.

And his house was empty again.

"It's nothing, Brit," he lied. "I'm fine."

"Bullshit," she said. "I can see it on your face, Will. What's going on?"

He went quiet for a long moment, gaze on his hands, debating. Brit was good at fixing things. And she enjoyed it—hell, some might even say she was obsessed with it. So, Will knew she'd jump on the opportunity to fix his problems.

But...he'd fucked up.

He needed to be the one to fix it.

Even if every single fucking time he closed his eyes, he saw Lily's naked body, her flushed cheeks, her *hurt* eyes.

"Look," he finally managed, giving Brit the truth. Because she wouldn't stop pushing if he tried to peddle bullshit, but also because she had a big heart and a shitload of empathy and she *cared*. "I'm not ready to talk about it."

She didn't miss a beat. "You should—"

"I'm *not* ready to talk about it," he repeated.

"Will—"

He spun to face Brit—and subsequently caught Ben and Lucas listening in as well. "Christ," he muttered, clenching his jaw, forcing himself to hold each of their gazes in turn. "Yes, it's about a woman." He shook his head when Brit went to speak. "Yes, it's fucking with my head." His eyes narrowed when she practically wiggled with impatience to weigh in. "No, I don't want to talk about it, or need any help with it, or want you fuckers poking your noses in it." A breath as he strived for calm and patience. Then he added, "No offense meant."

Brit's mouth tipped up, eyes dancing. "None taken."

She fell silent after that.

Thank fuck.

But it only lasted for a couple of heartbeats.

Then a bit of wicked curled into the edges of her voice. "Are you sure?"

Will groaned, head dropping back to *thunk* against the wall.

"Just saying"—she was laughing now, teasing enough that he knew she'd drop the conversation...at least for now—"we're really good at fixing women problems."

He turned to look at her again. "I know."

———

"Thank you for your apology," Lily told him a few days later. "I appreciate it."

"Lil—"

"Nope. Not today, Will."

"Lily—"

"I said *not today.*"

And then she backed away, shut the door with a firm *click.*

Again.

Like she had every single day. After every single apology.

She accepted them, stayed distant while doing so, and then—somewhat politely—closed that fucking office door.

He sighed, knew he needed to regroup.

Lil hadn't begun meeting with players yet, but it was only a matter of time—and because he knew she wouldn't hesitate to do her job to the absolute best of her ability—he knew he'd have a meeting with her too.

That good be good.

A captive audience he could apologize to until he wore her down, until she forgave him.

He just...couldn't wait however long that would be to make things right between them.

He'd overreacted. He knew that. He'd been an asshole—and he seemed determined to continue on that path if her response to his apology was any indication.

Not one glimpse of a smile.

Not one inch of melt.

His fault—something he was fully aware of.

He just...

"Christ," he muttered, turning away and heading down the hall of the practice facility, away from the office she'd set up there as well. It would be her main space, the one in the arena reserved for any game day needs. He knew he was pushing, invading.

But at least he'd come before practice? Instead of after, or after a game and smelling like a cat that had been run over and left out to fester in the California sun.

Progress?

Sure. Whatever he needed to tell himself.

Because it didn't feel that way, and he knew he was an extra special brand of asshole because he'd lied to Don the night before about how well they were getting along, expounding on Lily's fitting in with the team.

And she was.

She'd been a freaking shining light at the team dinner the night before.

The Lily of old. Sweet and lovely and so fucking warm to everyone but him.

Because *they* weren't getting along.

Because he'd hurt her and couldn't seem to stop being a dick to her—mostly because every time she smiled or laughed or hell, even glared at him, *his* dick went hard and then he was full of...

Problems.

She was a problem, but he'd made it *her* problem and that wasn't fair.

And now he needed to fix it.

Because this polite, dismissive, *icy* Lily...

He couldn't do it.

She'd expertly avoided him at dinner and had done it so not one person would have picked up the ice shards she was tossing his way.

But he'd felt every single one of them land.

Spear through him.

He deserved to bleed. He just—

"You're a shit eavesdropper, you know that, right?" Will muttered, coming up behind Ben, who was trying to act as though he hadn't been peeping in on the tense exchange.

"You're going to be late for practice if you don't get dressed," Ben said, still staring at the rack of sticks.

"Nice try." He stepped closer, tried to keep his tone even. "What'd you hear?"

"Hear?" Ben snagged his stick, spun to face Will. "Nothing."

Eyes narrowing, Will opened his mouth.

"Nothing except that you two were exchanging some sharp words I couldn't discern. But," he added, glancing up into his friend's stark face, "I saw—can see—that whatever it was she said sliced you to ribbons."

Will inhaled. Let the exhale out slowly. "I'm fine."

An obvious lie.

But Ben wasn't Brit. He wouldn't push—not right in that moment, anyway. Not when Will probably looked fucking sick to his stomach.

"Who is she?" Ben asked instead. He hadn't been at the team dinner, hadn't gotten that glimpse of Lily Light.

Something that should have been a good thing.

One less person to possibly pick up on the tension between him and Lily.

Except, Ben was *here*, and he'd seen—

Fucking hell.

"Lily Cartwright," Will said, going for cool and neutral and no big deal. "She's the sports psychologist that management just hired."

And failing.

Because Ben's expression was searching, his question quiet, "And who's she to you?"

He could lie.

But Ben had already seen.

So, he inhaled then let it out slowly, and admitted the truth that had been growing in his belly from the moment he'd realized it was her in the airport, "Everything."

TWELVE

LILY

Her phone rang, and she let it go through to voicemail.

Because it was her mom.

Because it was late enough that she shouldn't still be in her office, so she was going to pretend she was at home and in bed and—

A knock on the doorframe had her bleary eyes lifting from the screen of her cell to the open doorway.

Will was standing there. "Hey," he said softly.

"Hey," she whispered.

And braced.

Waited for the asshole to emerge, for whatever stick had been up his butt since she'd hit San Francisco to make a reappearance.

It didn't.

Instead, he strode forward and set a mug on her desk.

"I heard you're addicted to the chai." Still soft. Still without the asshole in sight.

She *was* addicted to the chai.

Mostly because one of the perks of this job was the kitchen. Or *kitchens*, as they were. It was a kitchen only loosely in definition—a sink, microwave, a couple of coffee makers. One of those pod ones where she could just jam in a canister, hit the button, and go, and another fancy machine with knobs and presses and all sorts of intimidating gauges. Luckily for her, Mandy had given her the rundown on day one—and she'd retained enough knowledge to steam milk. Thus, her obsession with chai lattes had begun. She could make them. They were delicious. And it was tea —she could pretend she was being healthy.

Why was this important?

Because it also enabled her addiction to the contents of the boxes of fresh pastries from a local bakery called Molly's that took up space on the counter next to that fancy machine.

Lil would be worried about getting fat, solely from her consumption of carbs—and chai lattes—if not for the fact that she was running around like a chicken with her head cut off.

Over to the practice facility. Back to the arena. Attending various team events. Hauling her tired body back to her apartment. Then back to her office early the next morning.

And rinse and repeat.

She had months to make up for.

She had a certain player to not focus on.

She had—

"I can take it back if you don't want it," Will murmured.

Lil blinked and glanced up from the steaming mug. He was shifting from foot to foot in front of her, eyes on his feet.

Very much *not* like the Will she knew.

"No," she said quickly. "I want it."

His eyes shot up, and she gave him a chagrined smile. "Calories don't count if they come in chai form."

His lips curved. "Is that right?"

She nodded, got lost in that gorgeous little smile for a couple of seconds, in the way the lock of hair fell across his forehead, and absently sipped the hot tea.

Delicious.

Maybe more than hers.

Probably because the man knew how to use that fancy machine—and more than just the steamer.

She sipped again, set the mug down, realized this was another chance to smooth things over. "I actually have something for you."

His brows lifted, lips curving further. "I like presents."

A giggle sliding off her tongue. "I'm not so sure you'll like this one." She pulled out the file she'd been creating for him. "It's homework."

His expression dimmed slightly, but proving that he was still at least partly the Will she knew, he nodded gamely. "Sock it to me."

She passed it over.

He flicked through the pages. "All the guys are going to do this?"

Worry started clawing at the edges of her belly. "Do you think they won't want to?"

He closed the folder, studied her. "Will it help you do your job?"

Well, yeah. She wasn't exactly going to have the guys do busy work.

"It'll help you," he said softly.

"Yeah." Lil lifted her mug, took a sip.

"Then the guys will do it."

Her brows came up. "That easy?"

He nodded. "That easy."

"Oh," she whispered.

"Yeah," he whispered back.

Silence fell between them again, and she searched for something to say, something to put him at ease. But she'd already thanked him for the drink and given him the homework. She didn't have any other high points to hit on her Will Agenda.

And she couldn't close the door on him to put an end to this awkwardness, not with him already in the room.

So...she just sipped.

Until the mug was empty and he was still standing there, staring at her.

"Right," she whispered, setting it back onto her desk. "I should let you get on—"

He was suddenly close, suddenly in her space, bending so that his face was only millimeters from hers.

Breath catching, she clung to the armrests of her chair, fingers digging into the plastic. "What—"

His hand came up.

His thumb brushed lightly over her top lip. "You have a little—"

Heat in her belly. Her pulse skittering in her veins.

He held up his thumb, showing her that the tip was covered in foam.

"I—"

He lifted it to his mouth, flicked out his tongue, and fuck if she didn't feel that between her legs.

"Will," she whispered.

Molten blue eyes. A spicy male scent in her nose. The bristles of his beard calling out for *her* to touch, and she didn't have the excuse of wiping foam off his lip.

"I know," he whispered back.

How silence could be hot, she didn't know. But it was. It scorched the air in her lungs, settled heavy in her belly, stroked heavily against her skin.

And Will was still right there.

No. He was *closer.*

Still so damned close and touchable and—

Her phone rang.

He jerked, so hard he nearly ended up on his ass, eyes flaring with panic.

"Will," she whispered.

"I'll get this filled out for you," he blurted, scrabbling for the papers, tucking them under his arm.

"I—"

His goodbye hit her ears before he'd even reached the door.

Then he was out of it.

Awkward. Tense. But...minus the asshole.

So...progress?

———

The chai on her desk the following evening after the game surprised her.

It probably shouldn't have.

Will was...well, he needed to take care of people, and as she reviewed the packet she'd sent home with him—completed expediently and dropped off before the game that evening because that was Will as well (responsible and getting shit done)—she'd also come to a deeper understanding of that.

He was a caretaker.

A people pleaser.

Conflict was more disruptive to him—and his game—than she'd anticipated.

A sneaky people pleaser.

Who brought her chai lattes and neatly completed homework.

"Damn," she whispered, internalizing that, along with the fact that tonight's game had been his best since she'd arrived in San Francisco. Which meant that it was time for her to divorce her emotions from her job.

For both of their livelihoods.

For the team itself.

He'd...what? Gotten turned on because he'd seen her naked and that didn't fit into the nice little box she was supposed to be stored in his mind?

Maybe?

He didn't want to start something with her because she was supposed to be the equivalent of his little sister?

Possibly.

He wanted to take care of her, and she was a grown woman who didn't need that kind of care?

Could be.

That or a combination of all of those things.

Lily hadn't figured it out yet. She would, though, and in the meantime, she'd accept the chai lattes and give him more homework and find a way to make sure his game wasn't affected by whatever nonsense was swirling in his head, that he wasn't in a self-fulfilling loop that continued to mess with his head and, potentially, with his place on the team.

She'd be patient.

And she'd accept *all* the chai lattes.

Poor her.

Thirteen

He held the chai latte in his hand, thankful that all the drinks had melted the ice wall Lily had erected.

Though he also assumed it was because he'd managed to not be an asshole for two whole weeks.

Today, he'd stolen an apple tart from the bakery box, intending to up his bribery tactics.

He'd noticed she went for the apple sweets, something he'd filed away in the previous days. Something he'd taken advantage *that* day, having finished some off-ice training earlier than usual, thus having the opportunity to raid the kitchen and full box of treats for Lily's favorite.

The team had been playing well—and thank fuck, he was too —so they'd mostly gotten a reprieve from the hard shit. He'd just needed to come in for some weights and conditioning and a few special exercises the trainers and Fanny, their skating coach, personalized for each of them.

He'd done that.

And now it was time for tea and sweets.

But when he went to her office in the practice facility—something he'd noticed she spent a shit-ton of time in—the desk was empty.

That was a good thing, he knew, even though disappointment sat heavy in his stomach.

She'd been working too hard.

Leaving the office at a reasonable time was a good start for her work-life balance. Not that he was going to tell her that, or advise her of that, or well, comment on *any* of her habits.

He was slowly dragging himself into her good graces.

He could leave commenting on her work schedule until his pro column was weighted a bit heavier.

Taking the mug with him, he turned from her office and went back to the kitchens to dispose of it. Because he sure as shit wasn't going to drink it. Lil's "Christmas in a mug"—and yes, that was a direct quote from a couple nights before when he'd decided to try it—had made him promptly want to wash the soapy taste out of his mouth.

Coffee was his jam.

But when he walked into the kitchen, expecting it to be empty like it had been when he'd left it less than five minutes before, it was to see Lil at the espresso maker.

He grinned, started to hold up the mug and apple tart. "I've got you cov—"

Any joking words he'd summoned froze on his tongue when she jerked around, and he saw her face.

"Lil." *Shit.* He dropped the mug and pastry on the table and moved toward her, taking her shoulders in his hands. "What's wrong, baby?"

She blinked, fingers tightening around the mug she held. "I'm fine. I-I—"

A tear slid down her cheek.

He drew her closer. "*Lil.*"

"I-I'm fine—"

But she wasn't fine.

Because she no sooner got the word out than she burst into tears.

———

He was used to female tears—God knew his mom had cried enough of them throughout his childhood that he should be immune to them.

But Lily's—

God, they were awful.

As though they were tearing her in half, ripping her to shreds.

"I-I—" Sobs wracking through her frame, shaking her so violently that he seriously worried he wouldn't be able to hold her together. "I-I-I'm f-fine. I-I-I—"

"Shh," he told her. "Don't try to talk. Just let it out."

But honestly, he wasn't sure that was the best advice. She'd been crying for so long that he'd begun to seriously worry.

That she wouldn't stop.

That something terrible had happened.

That Don or Val or Ted had—

"I-I'm o-okay."

He didn't argue with her, just kept running his hand up and down her spine, holding her close. The floor was cold and hard beneath his ass, but her weight in his lap was negligible. Hell, it was...right.

Perfect.

Something he shouldn't be thinking about, least of all right then.

"I'm..." She sucked in a long, trembling breath. Then released it slowly. "I'm—" She glanced up at him with reddened eyes. "You know about my last job? The trial?"

His heart sank. "Your dad might have mentioned it."

Her lips twitched. Slightly.

But then the anguish slid back into her eyes, and the curve of humor left her mouth. And her words...they sliced as deeply as those sobs had. "They decided to drop the charges," she whispered.

Every muscle in his body went ramrod stiff. "What?"

"I don't know what happened or if they paid the families off, but"—a shaking breath—"I got the call this evening."

"Lil."

She pushed off his lap, moved to the sink, and he listened to the water turn on as he rose to his feet. By the time he got there, she was splashing water over her face.

"Here," he murmured, extending a towel when it appeared she'd finished.

"Thanks," she whispered.

He took the damp towel, dropped it in the dirties basket, then wove his fingers through hers, grabbing the mug and pastry in his other hand. Then he drew her forward, out of the kitchen, away from where prying eyes might see.

Probably, he should take her back to her office, but that wasn't entirely private.

Someone could interrupt and—

He turned right, towing her along, and it was a statement of how upset she was that she didn't protest as he led her to one of the few private places in the practice facility.

It was just a quiet corner, a space he could pause and think and not be interrupted while he got his head straight.

But it would work in a pinch, give her some private time to sort herself out.

He drew her through the door, plunked her down onto the chair he'd smuggled in, dropping down in front of her and handing her the mug.

"Drink," he ordered softly when she just stared at the contents like she'd never seen tea before.

She drank deeply, so he decided to push it and passed her the pastry.

"Eat." Another order, but she was still out of it enough that she began nibbling.

"Apple?" she said after a few moments.

"Yeah, baby," he murmured. "I know they're your favorite."

That got him her eyes, and an apparent return to reality because they immediately went sad again.

"Will you tell me?" he asked gently.

"Why I'm a mess?" she countered.

"Yup. That."

"Will you take jet lag and working too much as an answer?"

He tugged a lock of her hair. "Nice try."

Her armor fell, eyes filled with anguish that sliced him deep.

"You're a good person," he whispered. "And I know the news would upset anyone and upset someone who worked closely with the kids even more. But you're..."

"Not just upset," she finished, the words barely audible. Her next ones were clear, though. "I was broken." A shake of her head. "I...I guess it's because I *feel* broken."

"I—" His teeth snapped together, his gut churning. Don had told him otherwise, but— "Did he hurt you too?"

Her eyes flared with pain. "Not the way you're thinking." She rubbed her forehead, sighed, and set the barely touched pastry on her lap. "I failed them, Will. They were mine to look after, and I couldn't do *anything* except stand by and—"

He took her hand when she didn't go on. "And what?"

"All I did was stand by and watch them get hurt."

Fourteen

The memories were swirling in her mind, too big, too painful.

The temptation was to push them down, to lock them away.

Because there wasn't going to be an end to this nightmare. There wouldn't be justice. A happy ending that was only found in movies.

This was the real world.

"I know you, Lil," he said. "And I know you wouldn't do that."

Except she had.

She'd watched for a sign to intervene, had waited too damned long, and people had gotten hurt. People had—

She cut that thought off in its tracks.

It was one thing to lose it over the charges being dropped. She didn't need to rehash those memories. Not right in this moment.

"They were mine," she whispered. "You get that, right?"

He sucked in a breath.

"I know you do," she said softly. "Because you're like me."

"Yeah, Lil, I am. I get why you'd have their backs, why you'd put it all on the line for them. You're a protector."

"Takes one to know one," she quipped, going for light.

Except, the joke didn't land.

Probably because she felt raw inside.

"I'm getting that." He took the mug from her and set it on the floor. "So, I know that no matter what I say, you'll feel like you left the job incomplete. And I know a lot," he added as her pulse began to speed up. "I heard exactly how far you pushed it. I heard what you did for those girls and how you stood up to that asshole and reached out to their parents. I heard how you were responsible for the news to break in the media and the subsequent conversations that took place in living rooms all across the world." He shifted closer, one warm hand resting on her knee, not helping her pulse situation. "I know you. And I know what it's like to feel responsible for others. But, pixie, you *helped* people. By not covering it up, by pushing the issue. By fighting for those girls."

"And in the end, it doesn't matter."

And, God, how deeply she felt that, *knew* that.

But also, God, how she wished she'd kept that particular fact to herself.

Because his face...yeah, he knew too much, saw too much, meant too—

He exhaled, fingers tightening on her knee. "I think some of them will recognize what you did, baby—"

Baby.

And seriously, so *not* helping her pulse.

But the fact remained. "The girls either think I deliberately ruined their dream by getting their coaches in trouble and putting the program in peril or they know the truth."

"Which is?" he asked after a moment.

"That I didn't do nearly enough to protect them."

Those fingers tightened further.

"How could that possibly be the truth?"

"It— " Lil pulled in a breath, thoughts and memories and

emotions swirling. She shouldn't be discussing this. She should be focused on the team and the way he was playing. But...she told him the rest of it anyway. Told him about the months of worry. The notes she'd kept. The way she'd desperately tried to get the parents on board. The abuse and the upheaval and how *her* dream had become something else.

Had become a nightmare.

"And what was it for?" she whispered. "All of that, and I might as well have done nothing."

"Except, you couldn't do nothing," he whispered back.

Damn the man. He knew her.

"No, I couldn't," she agreed.

He sighed and sank back on his heels. "So yeah, sweetheart," he murmured. "I know you're like me."

She scowled.

He grinned. "Is that so bad?"

"No," she muttered. "Except for the fact that *I'm* supposed to be the one who is insightful and put together and solves everyone else's problems."

"Something like a contractor's house is never fixed?" he quipped.

Another scowl. "I hate that analogy."

"Because it's true?"

She pursed her lips.

His mouth quirked up at the edges.

And her heart melted, just a little bit. "You're the same, you know?"

"A protector?"

"No. Well, yeah," she grumbled. "But that wasn't what I meant."

"Then what?"

"I *meant* that you're a pain in my ass."

He grinned. "Yup."

She swatted him with the napkin the pastry had been

wrapped in, getting crumbs everywhere. "I liked you better when I was mad at you."

"No, you didn't," he said with a boyish smile that settled deep in her belly.

"Ugh," she muttered.

He waggled his brows. "Will you feel better if I bribe you with more pastries?"

The man...*gah*, when he smiled at her like that—all cat-ate-the-canary—she went melty inside and forgot all about the asshole and remembered...

Fun times.

Sweet things.

Chai lattes and flaky pastries.

Friendship. A crush, however one-sided.

She didn't touch on anything, just nodded and said simply, "Yup."

And then he laughed, and it was awesome and her melty was filled with butterflies and—

"Is this—?" She frowned, finally fully taking in her surroundings. "Did you...bring me to a broom closet?"

He grinned, nudged her leg. "Shh. Don't look around. Just enjoy my special quiet corner and eat your pastry."

There were brooms. And shelves. And a single door. No windows.

She grinned.

So totally a broom closet.

Except with a cozy chair.

And pastries.

———

"Okay," Lucas said the following week, his eyes on the page, brows furrowed as he concentrated. "I can definitely try some of these."

"Just remember," she told him, leaning back against her desk, pleased that he was happy with her plan, "this is only a starting point. Though, I do think some of those techniques could help in managing the stress of everything happening at home."

That being his parents getting divorced.

That being this grown man coming to her because he wanted advice and help and—*squee!* She was helping one of her hockey players without dragging them forward by the ear.

"Yeah," he said, "I get that. I'm more worried about my sisters"—younger, still living at home, significantly more upset about the change in relationship status than Lucas was—"can they use some of these too?"

"Absolutely," she told him. "I'll forward that to your email, and you can decide the best way to share it. I think offering some suggestions of what works for you is a good place to start."

He tapped the papers on the desk, stacking them neatly. "Thanks, Doc. This is great."

Lil straightened off her desk. "I'm not technically a doctor, you know that, right?"

A flash of a sexy, confident smile—and damn, she liked that he'd come and sought out her help—almost as much as she liked the easy way he seemed to deal with everyone around him.

Time would tell if that steady would hold, or if it was a mask hiding some demons.

For now, though, he was on the right track.

But she was still keeping an eye on him.

"I know you're not a doc, Doc." He grinned. "But you're still one to us."

She narrowed her eyes. "Who's us?"

That smile didn't dim—even though she'd given him her most warning of tones. "Me. The guys."

"Is this some sort of hazing thing?"

A lazy shrug. "Nah, that's not the Gold way. Though," he added when she started to round her desk, intending to shut down her laptop and get her things together so she could go home. She had some reality TV to catch up with and leftovers from her most recent DoorDash culinary extravaganza.

A perfect night.

She paused, glanced up at him. "Though?" she asked archly when he didn't go on.

"The Gold way includes nicknames."

She lifted her brows. "Why am I scared?"

That smile again. "You shouldn't be. *Doc*," he added, making it clear the name wasn't going to go away.

Still, she asked, "That's not going away, is it?" She tapped at her keyboard, sending her laptop into sleep mode, and snagged her cell.

"Nope."

"Great," she muttered.

He chuckled.

"I guess I should be happy that I ended up with something innocuous?"

"Damn right." Wicked in his eyes. "You could have ended up like Axel, being called Balls."

She shouldn't laugh.

But...hell if the guys weren't funny.

So, she gave in. She laughed, and also got to appreciate the husky rumble of Lucas's amusement in turn.

"I think I'll stick with Doc," she said lightly.

"Good plan." A wink. "Doc?" he asked as she reached for her purse.

Her sigh was audible. "Yeah?"

"Want to grab dinner?"

She had leftovers and reality TV waiting for her at home...but she had Lucas in front of her, sweet and nice and with—one look at his face told her as much—what was a genuine offer of friendship and camaraderie.

Another invite into the Gold family.

The leftovers could wait.

So could her show.

"Dinner sounds great."

FIFTEEN

"I'm sorry, baby boy," his mom said. "I don't think I'll be able—"

"It's okay," he said quickly, gut souring, suddenly tired of this.

Again.

"It's just that we're recording an episode of the podcast and then Miriam needs my help..."

He sucked in a silent breath, held it long enough for his lungs to burn. Maybe the burn in his lungs would ease the burn in his gut.

Except, he knew it wouldn't.

"I get it, Mom," he told her, letting her off the hook because... what other option did he have? If he pushed the issue, she spiraled and still didn't come. If he didn't, she didn't come, but the drama stayed buried. And sometimes...she *did* come, did show. Which was why he kept asking. "Don't worry about it. The team plays the day after Christmas"—or two days after anyway, but she wouldn't check, wouldn't know any different—"so you might as well stay home and not fight the holiday crush to get yourself all the way out here."

Never mind that it was a four-hour flight, and he'd bought her a first-class ticket and—

This was his mother.

She did what she wanted, when she wanted, and...

Life.

That was life.

His life.

"If you're sure you'll be okay on your own, my baby boy," she said.

"I'll be fine," he assured her. It was true. He was always fine. "The team will keep me busy, anyway, and I'm sure Miriam needs you."

"She does!" his mom exclaimed, rustling in the background telling him that she was working. "She's hopeless when it comes to mixing colors and she promised her daughter she'd paint a mural on the nursery wall, and she can't have the giraffes be the wrong color of brown."

"No," he said, plunking his beer onto the counter, his excitement over his weekly Cheat Day—and subsequent Cheat Day Beer—evaporating like a certain team's playoff hopes. "Definitely can't have the wrong brown giraffe."

"Exactly!" More rustling in the background. Then a knock. "I've gotta go, baby."

"Right, Mom," he muttered.

A pause.

"You're mad." Worry had crept into her tone. Which would then turn into hurt. A dash of hysteria. And tears.

He was used to them.

But Lily's had left him with a gaping hole for the past week.

He'd left her smiling, had brought her treats and chai lattes every day their schedules had overlapped, but...Lily—his *Lily*— had been hurt, and—

Her face.

It had been like in the bathroom. When he'd—

A sniffle.

"I'm not mad," he said quickly, focusing on the problem he could solve at that moment. "I promise, Mom. I get it."

He did.

He had to.

Or it would make him go insane.

The knock on his mom's end came again.

"Not mad," he repeated. "Now answer the door, okay? We'll talk soon."

Him making her feel better. Her spinning and spinning. *Always* spinning. But better like this—spinning by flitting from one thing to the next rather than spinning down and out and—

Leaving him to pick up the pieces.

"I want to see pictures when you guys are done," he added to keep her on track.

"I—" She still sounded unsteady. "But we're just sketching tonight."

"I'd like to see those too."

"Really?"

Like a little girl pleasantly surprised that she'd pleased her father.

Then again, that was more of the same.

It was a fucking miracle his mom had survived her childhood, had survived Will's father. It just...sometimes it would have been nice if she could be the parent and him the kid. If she'd think about what he wanted, what he needed...and not what she wanted.

"Really," he said softly.

"Okay, great," she chirped, spiral assuaged and flitting on to the next thing. "Talk to you soon, my baby."

"Bye—"

The call disconnected.

He looked at his phone, at his half-drunk beer, at his empty kitchen.

Then pushed off the stool and got the fuck out of his sad, empty house.

Or maybe it was out of his sad, empty life.

———

In retrospect, Mafia's had been a bad idea.

There was always a Gold player there on a Cheat Day, and tonight wasn't any different.

Lucas, Rome, and Ben were sitting around a table.

Worse?

Lily was here.

His Lily.

Who was cuddled up to Rome of all people. And fuck, the only one worse to be cuddled up next to would have been Lucas, who was allergic to commitment.

Rome played the field, but Will knew he had a thing for a certain vineyard owner's daughter.

Who'd turned him down and—

Not Will's business.

He turned to leave, but—*of fucking course*—they'd noticed him.

"Will!" Lucas called. "Come over, man!"

He ground his teeth together but moved to the table. He hadn't been able to stand staying in his house after his mom had flaked on him again—this time for fucking Christmas.

And now he had the feeling he wasn't going to be able to stand sitting at this table.

He was...raw.

Vulnerable.

Disappointed.

Again.

These men, this family that had obliquely become his, would see too much. And so would Lily. More so because it was her job, and she knew him from before and...

He didn't want to think about that.

His feelings for her were complicated and confusing and something he couldn't explore.

Not when he'd promised her dad he'd look after her. Not when he'd finally smoothed things over between them. Not when—

"Umm, Will?" Ben asked.

He blinked, glanced down and realized he was at the table, had made it to the table locked in his own thoughts.

"You gonna sit down?" Ben's brows lifted.

Ben was cool. He had a girlfriend, and they were serious. But he wasn't oblivious.

And he was looking at Will like he'd lost his goddamned mind.

And maybe he had.

Because when he looked at the other two fuckers...sandwiching Lily—*his* Lily—he wanted to—

Laughter in the air, sweet, soft *Lily* laughter filling the space between him and his friends.

Fucking hell.

"Sit, man," Ben ordered, snapping him out of it.

Fuck, man. Get your shit together.

He sank down into the booth, reaching for Rome's beer and taking a huge sip.

"Hey!" Rome grumbled.

Will just took another swallow. If the fucker he'd considered a friend was going to sidle up to Lily, then he was going to pay in beer.

Because—sweet fucking God—his teammates (minus Ben) were staring at Lily like she was the last fry in the giant basket of fried potato deliciousness in front of her.

They'd devour her.

They'd hurt her.

They'd—

No, they fucking *wouldn't.*

He drank deeper, shooting Rome a glare when he shifted closer to Lily, tilting his phone so she could better see what was on the screen, better see what had caused her laughter to bubble up and fill the space between them. Will had forgotten about that laughter, how light and sweet and *wonderful* it was. It was like standing under the first warm rays of sunshine after a storm.

Which, of fucking course, had him wanting that same feeling to be settling on his naked skin, *Lil* pressed to him and enjoying the sensation too.

Her laughter was something that Rome was apparently drawn to as well.

Because Lil's laughter had his annoying-as-fuck teammate moving closer, until their shoulders were touching and he unleashed a panty-dropping smile. *Fucker.* Lily had an empty wineglass in front of her. And Rome's beer had been mostly empty before Will had commandeered it.

Which meant they'd both been drinking.

Which meant she might not make the best decisions.

For her.

Not for Will. His opinion didn't weigh in on this and—

She shifted, moved so she was even closer to his teammate, looking up at Rome through lowered lashes. And smiled.

Christ.

The absolute last thing she needed was to hook up with a player who had no interest in settling down. She'd get her heart broken, and Lil had been through enough.

"Can I get you guys anything else?"

He opened his mouth, intending to ask for a menu, knowing he was here for the long haul.

He'd see Lily home. Without Rome.

"Can I have another glass of wine?" Lily asked.

Fuck. Her cheeks were flushed—from Rome, from the wine she'd already had.

The server smiled, started to nod and turn away.

"No."

The word flew off his tongue well ahead of his brain, every instinct in his body screaming, "No more booze! No more Rome!"

Four sets of shocked eyes slid toward him, including the server's, who was staring at him totally aghast. "I..." He balked. Fuck. He was an idiot. "I mean, I-I—" he stammered for an explanation that didn't make him sound like the biggest asshole on the planet. "It's late and I-I—" He glanced over at Lily. "I mean, shouldn't you go to bed?"

She glanced at her watch. "It's six-thirty."

"But"—he scrambled for a reasonable explanation, for any reasonable excuse to get her away from Rome and his panty-dropping abilities—"you've been working long hours and y-you must be tired."

"I'm fine." She smiled at the waiter. "And I'll have that glass of wine. Thanks."

Will should have just shut up.

He *should* have.

But then Rome shifted even closer.

And Will found himself blurting, "Don't you want something else instead of wine? Like a..." He kept scrambling, trying to think of something. Luckily—no, *stupidly*—inspiration struck. "A Shirley Temple. You still like those, right?"

Sixteen

Lily

A Shirley Temple.

Instead of a glass of wine.

What the fuck was happening right now?

She'd thought they were past the asshole.

The only positive from Will's obvious declaration that he still saw her as a fucking child who couldn't be trusted to know her limits enough to drink a couple of glasses of wine, was the fact that his teammates were as aghast as she was.

"A fucking Shirley Temple, man?" Rome asked, his cell dropping to his thigh. "What is she, six?"

"Fuck you, man," Will muttered. "People like Shirley Temples."

"Yeah, and they're *six*," Lucas chimed in before he glanced at her, smiling softly, his hazel eyes as warm as they'd been from the moment he'd first walked into her office, looking for help. "Drink *all* the wine, sweetheart. Life's too short to not indulge every now and then."

She grinned at him. "Thanks, Luc."

He winked at me then nodded at the server, who wisely took the opportunity to escape.

"And don't worry about Will," Rome said, scrolling to another video on his phone—and while she was finding the videos funny, she wasn't enjoying the vibes she was getting from Will that came from her leaning close enough to properly see them on Rome's cell. Plus, she was feeling more than a little rude, all but ignoring Lucas and Ben while staring at a phone screen.

"True," Ben added, clearly not upset about her ignoring them in lieu of funny TikTok videos. "He's just old and cranky."

Will *was* old—at least probably to baby-faced Rome.

Will was also giving off major vibes.

Asshole vibes.

Controlling vibes.

Again. She glanced away from the cell's screen and up at Will, whose conflicted expression had her tabling her irritation.

What was going on with him?

She knew her dad had pushed him to watch out for her. Maybe he resented that she'd infiltrated his life? Except, he didn't seem to feel that way when he was bringing her chai lattes and treats. Or when he'd comforted her about the charges being dropped.

His eyes came back to hers and the conflict in his blue irises, in the grooves on either side of his mouth, had her going still.

What the hell?

But the twitching muscle in his jaw told her he wasn't going to be open for another heart-to-heart.

Not when that would mean *he* needed the one who was vulnerable.

"Why shouldn't I worry about Will?" she asked, breaking the connection of their gazes and glancing back at Rome.

"Circling back to old." Rome snatched his beer back, took a sip. "And cranky."

"I'm not old," Will muttered. "I'm not even thirty yet."

"Getting close," Ben pointed out.

"Not *that* close."

She grinned.

He glared. "It's not funny."

"That you're clearly worried about approaching thirty?"

The guys laughed.

"It's *definitely* funny," said with a grin.

He scowled, the expression deepening when the server came back with her glass of wine. Though, thankfully, he didn't comment further on her alcohol consumption.

"Are you eating?" Ben asked, way too innocently. "Or brooding?"

Lil snorted.

Okay, well, she *tried* to hold it back—something that was an epic failure based on the glare Will tossed her way. But he still didn't comment on the teasing, just dutifully ordered a burger and beer, and Rome got a refill, and the atmosphere relaxed—though, she noticed that mostly came when she shifted away from Rome.

They talked about nothing important—the team and the upcoming Christmas break and the team's prospects for the playoffs.

And somehow, she found herself admitting, "You know this is embarrassing, but I used to have a crush on him." She smiled over at the broody mofo—growing broodier by the second—and winked. "*Used* to being the operative word."

Will glowered.

Looks were exchanged around the table.

Rome's mouth hitched up. Ben's and Lucas's followed suit.

"What?" she asked, genuinely confused.

Rome shrugged, turned away from Ben to meet her eyes, his dancing with humor. "Did you write his name in your diary too?"

"Every single night." She smothered a smile, mostly because Will growled. Again. Then added dryly, "Mrs. Shirley Temple Johansson."

The table exploded with laughter.

Will glowered.

She laughed—even though that wasn't a lie (minus the Shirley part)—thankful it had been enough years so that she could poke fun at herself.

Rome slid her wine glass closer. "Imbibe." A grin. "Then tell us more, Doc."

Three heads bobbled.

Lucas picked up his glass, took a long swallow. "We need *all* the dirt on *Shirley*."

"That better not stick," Will muttered.

"Oh, it's sticking," Ben said.

"Damn right it is, *Shirley*," Rome added. "Now"—he turned to Lily—"we need to know every embarrassing detail you know about him."

"Despite the fact that I haven't lived with him for near on a decade?"

A shrug. "Old embarrassing facts are still embarrassing."

She couldn't fault the logic in that, but still, this man—*Will*, that was—had brought her treats and chai and—

"Don't worry about *Shirley*," Rome told her, nudging his shoulder against hers, ignoring Will when he glowered again. "Just give us the goods."

So, she gave them the Cliff's Notes about Will living with them for a year as a billet player. Then gave them the goods—or the rest of them, anyway. "He and my brother, Ted, tag-teamed to destroy my middle school social life." She arched a brow at Will. "Based on his reaction to my second glass of wine, I'm guessing that instinct to treat me like I'm made of porcelain hasn't changed."

"I didn't destroy anything," he muttered. "I just wasn't going to let that ass Ricky Montanan think that he could take you behind the gym and—"

She balled up her napkin and tossed it at him. "Did you ever think that, perhaps, I *wanted* Ricky to take me behind the gym and kiss me?"

He shuddered. "God, no. That kid had a butt cut."

"I *liked* his hair."

Will rolled his eyes. "Drink your wine."

She picked up her wine glass and took a sip—not because he'd ordered her to, but because she was thirsty, dammit. "Have you forgotten that I'm a grown woman?"

"Oh, yeah?" he asked dryly. "Is that so?"

Her chin came up. "Yeah, Will," she said, feeling the sting of that question. "I am."

She watched his face change. Braced.

"Have you forgotten that you can't even keep track of your *towels?*"

She sucked in a breath at the sharp accusation, and suddenly *this*—the teasing and hanging out, the reminiscing of the *old days* —wasn't the least bit fun.

It was...

Her gaze drifted from Will's, honed in on the three sets of eyes that were ping-ponging between her and the brooding hockey player sitting across from her.

Done.

"I thought we'd finished this," she whispered. "That you understood, and we'd moved on."

His hands were clenched into fists. "I do," he ground out. "*We* did."

Except...he hadn't, not if he was still bringing it up like it was the worst burden to bear to have seen her naked, as though she were a complication he didn't want in his life. An error in his perfect judgment.

And...her heart squeezed hard.

She couldn't do this, couldn't be *that.*

Not now. Not in this life. Not...with him. Not *ever* with Will.

Suddenly, this wasn't fun or sweet or making her feel like she was part of something special. She just...wanted to go.

Calmly, she set her glass down and extracted her wallet from her purse. "I'm going to call it a night." Her fingers closed around a handful of bills, and she started to tug them out, but Rome caught her hand, tucked the money back into her wallet. "Don't ruin a good exit, sweetheart," he murmured, leaning close, voice dropping as he whispered in her ear, "I got you."

Will growled.

And seriously, the fucking *gall* of the man.

But...Rome was right.

It was time for that exit.

Time to be done with this. With him.

She gave Rome a smile, tossed the same to Lucas and Ben.

Will, she didn't bother to acknowledge.

Instead, she pushed to her feet, tucked her purse over her shoulder, and slid from the booth, glad to get the hell out of there, vowing *that* was going to be the last time Will Johansson got anything that wasn't work-related from her.

———

"Hey, Mom," she murmured a few days later, rubbing her eyes and glancing at the clock, just now realizing how late it was. "No," she lied as worried words pounded over the speaker now pressed to her ear, "Of course I'm not still at the office. I was napping on my couch. Fell asleep on my show."

Liar, liar, she knew, willing her office door to stay firmly shut.

She'd been spending even more time here than usual—mostly to avoid thinking about her feelings. And yeah, feelings and functioning at full capacity and thinking through tricky situations were her superpowers.

It was just...

There'd better not be a single delivery of chai or pastries—or *Will*.

Christ, a Shirley Temple. Keeping track of her *towels*.

She smothered a sigh, knowing she was bordering on unhealthy habits by dwelling on it, fixating on the look in his eyes as he'd snapped at her and yet unable to stop herself. Especially, because...

Something wasn't right.

She almost didn't care about the asshole comments and the *losing track of her towels.*

Because something was wrong with him.

So did that make her a willing punching bag? Weak?

Did that mean she'd failed? Again? Allowing another asshole to take over her life, to use her like that punching bag?

Just because he hadn't seemed like himself and she wanted to help—

"No," she whispered.

Her mom paused in her soliloquy. "What's that, honey?"

"I—" A shake of her head. *Focus, Lil.* "I'm just thinking."

"Oh, good," her mom said. "Me too. About Christmas—"

Admittedly, she tuned out the talk of garland and cookie baking. Because she was fixating. On Will. On the determination in her belly. On believe she was *not* a failure. That she could make this work. The team. The guys. This job. That she'd figure out things with Will, sort through whatever was going on in his head. Yeah, she'd started on the job late and she was still behind where she wanted to be. But if she just worked hard enough, she could make sure they were all ready for the push that would be the second half of the season.

It was just...it had to be done this week because she'd been roped into something called a Pie Extravaganza on the weekend and based on the emails and excitement and sheer number of mentions from players and staff alike, she knew it was going to be a big deal.

Honestly, a Pie Extravaganza sounded perfect.

Maybe the carb coma would help her sleep again, would help her to stop thinking about Will's face at dinner and—

Anyway, she'd been told to bring something green...that wasn't Jell-O. Which Lil figured was code for a salad. Since she was a hopeless cook, she was thankful for the fact that grocery stores had prepackaged bags of salad which meant all she had to do was dump everything into a bowl and slop some croutons and dressing on top to create her something green.

"I was wondering," her mom went on, and—*shit*—Lily really needed to focus on the conversation happening against her eardrum and not the one in her head. "I know you don't want us to come out, but are you sure you can't fly home? We're happy to buy you a ticket if things are tight."

God no.

Things were a *little* tight, thanks to that slightly more expensive apartment, but the Gold were paying her well enough that she was feeling okay, and that tight would get better because she wasn't actively depleting her savings.

She *could* afford a plane ticket.

It was just...she needed space, needed more time away from her parents so she didn't see their worry for her in their eyes.

Ever since the charges had been dropped, she'd been fielding calls and texts and *worry*.

Yeah, she'd freaked out a little bit.

Yeah, that was an understatement considering that Will had needed to corral her to a broom closet in order for her to regain control.

Will.

Something else that she didn't need them picking up on.

The tangle of emotions that was her situation with him.

He was still playing like shit—and she knew that was her fault. He probably felt guilty about the comments at dinner and whatever had put that look on his face—

"Will could come too!"

God, it was like her mom had radar for this shit.

"Mom," she began. "I'm sure he's busy."

"He's not. He just talked to your father last night and his mother"—she sneered the word, and Lil got it, Will's mother was...not made for the role of parenthood—"isn't going to fly out." A sharp sigh. "She isn't going to see her son on Christmas. I swear that woman's dreams are funded by Will. The least she could do was *pretend* to give a damn about him."

That explained part of his face—Will had always been heavily impacted by his mother's actions. Not that it was a surprise. His dad wasn't in the picture, and his mom was...well, his mom, and that impacted the way he interacted with people like *her* parents.

People he cared about. Like *her.*

Shit.

Pieces were clicking into place.

Half life.

Her parents filling a role in his.

Her not fitting into that neat, little box any longer and—

"So, anyway, I'm not going to take no for an answer," her mom said. "You both are going to fly out and—"

"Mom," Lil said, clutching the pencil she'd been writing with tightly enough that the wood protested. Because she was about to lie. Again. Either that or do something stupid.

Or...both.

"Will and I are going to spend Christmas together."

SEVENTEEN

"You've got crabs!" Brit cried.

"Come on, Shirley!" Lucas groaned, dropping his cards onto the table riddled with pie crumbs. "Pay the least bit of fucking attention, I've been signaling to you for the last five minutes."

Will glanced down at his cards, realized that he'd also had crabs (aka enough matching cards to signal Lucas back so they could attempt to win the round, but he'd been too in his own head to process that), and sighed. "Fuck," he muttered, tossing them on the table.

"Weakest link, man," Lucas grumbled.

Which...felt great, thank him very much.

"What are you doing with your mom for the holiday?" Brit asked, probably trying to throw him a bone, but unknowingly reopening a wound. "If you need some place to bring her, I'm sure Stefan would love a buffer between his parents and himself."

"Why?" Lucas asked, thankfully before Will had to come up with a reply to Brit's question.

"You know what they say about rekindled love." Brit

shrugged. "The PDA is off the charts, even for me"—a grin—"and *I* was rooting for them."

Everyone laughed.

Except Will.

His parents weren't like that. Hell, the only memory he had of his dad was blurry. And angry. And not at all like Brit's in- laws, whose love shone brightly every time they were in the room together.

"So anyway," Brit said, unfortunately returning to the previous topic at hand, "you'd be doing us a favor if you guys came by."

He tried for distraction. "Roxie isn't enough of a buffer?"

Brit's face lit up. "Roxie is the *best* buffer," she murmured. "But we always have room for more."

Which was why Will would do anything for them—*all* of these fuckers, despite their nosiness and their penchant for being too competitive over boardgames.

Anything...except admit that his life was empty.

Because his mom had flaked.

Again.

"Right," he said and pushed out of his chair. "We've got a packed schedule," he lied—sort of, because his mom was busy with the mural and podcast, and he had a positively slammed agenda of watching sports and playing video games and pretending to be okay. "But I'll let you know if things change."

Brit's eyes held his—long enough he thought she would call him on his bullshit—but then she nodded. "Okay, Will."

He retreated a step. "And since clearly I've had too much pie to properly play this game, Rome, you're up."

"Game time, baby!" Rome slid smoothly into the chair, and Will did his best to avoid the other set of eyes at the table. The pretty hazel ones that seemed to see too much.

He sighed, moved into the kitchen in search of something that wasn't pure sugar.

And found exactly one salad.

Mostly untouched—minus the candied walnuts Ben was picking out from amongst the leaves.

"What's doing, Shirley?" Ben asked, chomping loudly.

"Cute," he muttered.

A shrug as he grabbed another walnut, kept chomping.

"Well, aren't you a picture of an attractive male?" he asked dryly.

"So says the single one." A lifted brow. A smirk. "At least my girl is all in with me." A long pause that had Will's hackles lifting. "So...what's up with you and Lil?"

"Nothing."

"Hmm."

"*Nothing.*"

Ben didn't reply to the obvious lie, just grabbed another walnut. "You know—"

And right, *that* was the end of this conversation.

Will grabbed the bowl of salad, ignoring Ben's "Hey!" He held it against his chest as he escaped the party and stepped out onto the back deck.

But he couldn't ignore the feel of those hazel eyes as he went.

Nor the warmth and confusion that warred in his gut that came every time he was in the same room as her.

———

He'd helped clean up Brit's place after eating an obscene amount of pie.

But her house was sparkling, and he didn't have any other reason to delay heading home.

Not unless he wanted to admit his mom wasn't coming and he was alone and—

Yeah. That wasn't going to happen.

Lily had gone hours before, leaving before he'd reappeared after eating that entire bowl of salad with his bare hands.

And every one of the remaining candied walnuts.

Maybe a bit out of spite, but also because they were fucking delicious, so Ben knew that much at least.

Will had wanted to go then too, especially with Ben and Brit both studying him closely, but he'd forced himself to stay, to pretend to be happy and enjoying the festivities.

He was...and he wasn't.

Because all he'd been thinking about was his mom and being alone...and the tiny blond pixie who was driving him to insanity.

Absolute *fucking* insanity.

Who was responsible for the conflict turning his insides wrong side out.

The moment he'd picked her up at the airport everything had gone wrong.

Wrong.

Because she'd walked up to him, and he'd wanted to *claim*.

Fucking stupid.

Fucking dangerous.

Dangerous enough that he was spending all of his time pushing that desire out of his brain and shoving her firmly back into the metal box that was coded as sister.

Sister.

Completely and totally off-limits.

Not sexual.

Not touchable.

Not lickable or strokeable or fuckable.

Except that ass of hers...

His dick twitched.

"Fuck," he muttered, sending threats to the offending organ, advising it to behave, otherwise he'd punish it.

Something it didn't give a fuck about.

Because punishment meant jerking himself off until he was so drained that his dick couldn't get hard, even at the thought of sexy, pixie Lily.

His dick liked *that* punishment very much.

And hell, so did the rest of him.

But besides the attraction he couldn't act on, the bigger issue might be that he was talking to his dick, treating it like it was a whole different person.

"I'm out of here, everyone!" he called before he spiraled further.

Hands were waved in goodbye, hugs exchanged, and he managed to stop thinking about his dick and Lily for all of the fifteen minutes it took for him to drive home and pull into his garage, closing the large metal door behind him. Mostly because he was thinking about his mom and the podcast and the mural and the flaking. He'd thought he would grab a flight back home to Minnesota in a few days to surprise her, but then she'd texted him with a picture of her and Miriam in full creative mode.

There wasn't any point in flying home.

She'd be busy, and—

Well, if he was going to be alone, he might as well be alone in his own house. His own bed and food and couch.

So tomorrow, he'd spend Christmas Eve alone.

And then after that, Christmas Day alone.

And the days until he got back on the ice. Alone.

It wasn't a big deal. Will was used to spending lots of time by himself.

Or at least, that was what he told himself when the loneliness crept in, choking him, making his skin feel too tight for his body, making it hard for him to breathe.

He was used to that, too.

Single mom.

Kid at home alone a lot.

Hockey was a great outlet, but he couldn't horn in on his teammates every single day, even if they invited him. They had lives and kids and pets and women and PDA-obsessed in-laws.

So, he shoved the yearning down, breathed through the vice tightening around his lungs, and...he lived his life.

Tonight, though, he just wanted to go to bed. He wanted to sleep and forget about the loneliness and the fact that he would be spending Christmas alone with his Xbox and his palm, creating callouses from all the button pushing and jerking off. Maybe those behaviors weren't very much aligned with the holiday spirit, but that was what he had.

All that he had.

So as soon as the garage was closed up, he turned off the engine, got out, and slammed the car door.

He walked into his house.

Scrabbled along the wall until he found the switch—something he struggled with, even though he'd been living there for years now.

Finally, he felt the right switch, pressed it, and the kitchen lights flicked on.

And Will nearly jumped right the fuck out of his skin when he saw that Lily was sitting at his kitchen island.

Eighteen

Right.

So this might be a dumb idea.

Was *definitely* a dumb idea.

But his face during board games, the pieces clicking into place, her white lie to her mom that she'd had absolutely no intention of following through on...and she hadn't gone home when she'd left the Pie Extravaganza.

Nope.

She'd hit up Target.

And fought with a little old lady over the stash she'd carefully set up in the living room.

Then she'd waited.

An inordinate amount of time that she'd changed her mind during. Multiple times.

Because this was overstepping and dangerous and—

"Lil," he finally said after practically jumping a foot off the ground. "What the fuck?"

More nerves, but she pushed them down and tilted her head toward the living room. "Follow me."

Then she hurried into the other room, hustling across the space and plugging in the extension cord she'd commandeered from Will's mud room...

Just as he walked over the threshold.

She blinked at the sudden brightness, but only for a second, only for long enough that Will's face came back into focus. He'd frozen in place, eyes wide, big body still.

"What is this?"

Why was it that her words stoppered up in the back of her throat? That the explanation she'd wanted to give him wasn't coming?

Probably because he looked like she'd just railed him into the boards.

Head was down. Mind was rattled. Breath was stolen.

And then her words came.

"I brought Christmas," she whispered.

His eyes shot to hers.

Uncertainty coiled in her belly.

"I...um...my mom mentioned that your mom"—his expression clouded—"was um...busy for Christmas and wasn't going to be able to come out, so I..." She swallowed hard. "I wanted to bring some of the Christmas magic to you."

"Why?" he asked, stepping closer.

"Why?" she repeated, stomach twisting at the cold, soft question.

"Yeah," he murmured. "Why would you do this? I'm—" He broke off, gaze sliding to the side. "Because my mom isn't like yours, you feel sorry for me?"

Yes.

But...no.

She just...never wanted to see that broken expression on his face again, the one at the Pie Extravaganza, the one from thirty seconds before—and she wanted to do something nice for him, because even despite the Shirley Temple comments and occasional emergence of his inner asshole, he was a good guy.

Chai lattes.

Apple pastries.

Gently wiping her tears.

So...Christmas.

Or one that resembled Charlie Brown's and was the best she could do before Target closed and she'd had to bribe the little old lady for a hundred bucks for the last remaining tree that was currently listing in the corner, barely standing upright under the sparse array of garland and ornaments she'd managed to get into her cart. Only half the lights worked, but there were presents beneath, and she'd...

Well, she just wanted to do something nice for the man.

Was that a crime?

Did she have to dissect it into tiny, palatable pieces in her mind?

Yes! screamed her subconscious.

No! shouted her heart. *Just go with it.*

"I'm alone for Christmas, too," she said softly. "And I... wanted to spend it with you."

"Why?" he asked again.

It was tempting to blurt back "Why?" a second time, but she managed to take a breath, to line up the words in her mind.

"Because of Shirley Temples."

He blinked again, expression clouding. "What the fuck, Lil?"

"And chai lattes and apple pastries and comforting me when I was upset. And taking a hit on the ice that was intended for Ben because you wanted to give him a clear shot up the ice." He inhaled. "And calling my parents regularly and keeping up with Ted and loving your mom even though she doesn't always give that back."

An exhale.

"You take care of people," she whispered. "And you were trying to take care of me. I'm not saying it's my favorite thing"—she let her lips curve up—"or even on the list of my top favorites," she said. "But I get it, Will."

"You get it," he repeated.

"Yup." She smiled, moved to the tree and grabbed one of the presents she'd hastily wrapped. "You're my surrogate Ted, and it's not like I need another big bro, but I understand that's kind of your superpower, so I'll relax about it."

"Relax about me acting like an older brother."

There was something in his voice that didn't sit quite right, but she pushed on anyway, moving toward him. "Yup." She thrust the box at him. "But if you're going to be my big brother, then you need to indulge me like the little sister I am." She grinned. "All of which means Christmas traditions!"

His brows were up, and his eyes told her he thought she'd lost her mind.

But he took the box anyway, and she returned to the tree, grabbed the present she'd wrapped even more messily for herself, because this wasn't for her—not really, or not *totally*, anyway—and moved back to Will.

Who'd snapped out of his statue mode, somewhat anyway.

"Christmas traditions," he repeated slowly. "What does that mean exactly?"

"It means you open the present—"

"But it's not even Christmas yet."

She waved a hand. "This is a pre-Christmas present."

"Okay, so I open the pre-Christmas present"—she smiled, was relieved when his lips turned up in return—"and then what?"

"Then"—she nudged the box closer—"it's time for Christmas Traditions!"

This time she paired it with throwing her hands up with snowflake fingers and did the little dance she and her mom always did when the holidays came around.

Because it was fun.

Because it made them all laugh.

Because Will needed that.

Because hearing his rough chuckle had her heart leaping, thumping against her chest, her belly warming in a way that reminded her of the butterflies she'd had when she'd written Mrs. Lily Johansson over and over in her diary.

Surrounded by hearts and squiggles.

"Okay," he murmured.

"Okay?" She poked him lightly in the chest. "You'll stop being grumpy and fully participate in Cartwright Christmas Traditions?" she asked. "Even if you think they're stupid?"

"Do these traditions involve me doing something illegal?"

Her brows drew together. "Um...no?"

"Do they involve me acquiring more terrible nicknames?"

"I happen to like Shirley." She winked. "It goes with that hint of red in your beard."

He snorted.

She nudged the box again. "Just open your presie."

His eyes held hers and then he slid one finger down—and yes, she felt that big, rough digit between her thighs—hooked it beneath the edge of the paper, and tugged.

The wrapping ripped and he kept pulling, tearing until the paper was off and had dropped to the floor.

Only then did he glance down at the box and open the lid.

She was...nervous.

Oddly so.

Knowing she was pushing it, that he might hate, hate *them*, hate what she wanted to do—

But then he pulled out the present and started laughing. "Fuck." He laughed, holding up the only onesie she'd been able to get in his size (this being Teenage Mutant Ninja Turtles-themed —though at least it was Michelangelo, since he was the best). "I'd forgotten about this."

She smiled, tore into her own box and revealed her contribution to the festivities—Princess Peach. "New pajamas are Cartwright tradition, but the onesies are *our* addition." She set them on the couch, moved back to the tree. "But this is *the* tradition."

"Tell me you didn't."

She tossed the box to him. "I'm me. What do you think?"

He tore off the wrapping and grinned.

"Oh, yeah," he murmured. "Damn right you did."

Nineteen

Two mugs with dredges of hot chocolate sat on the coffee table, a huge bowl that had once held an obscene amount of popcorn and now just contained a few unpopped kernels at the bottom had been shoved next to them.

And he'd started the DVD again.

Because there was a warm weight against his side.

Lily, clad in a Princess Peach onesie that looked both fucking adorable and ridiculously sexy on her curvy body, her eyes closed, lashes shadowing the pale skin of her upper cheeks, her lips parted as she breathed slow and steady and deeply.

Somehow sleeping despite the explosions and gunshots.

Meanwhile, he was wide fucking awake, sweltering in his new tradition of fleece-hell pajamas, unwilling to shift even an inch to wipe the sweat that was dripping down his brows, threatening to get into his eyes.

He knew it would burn if it made it that far.

He still couldn't bring himself to move.

Because Lily was asleep and against him and...

He was at peace in a way he'd never been before—a way that

had his skin crawling and pulse pounding and panic eating away at his insides if he allowed himself to truly think about it.

Which he didn't.

Because...he couldn't move.

Because she was pressed to him.

And she'd...*fuck*. She'd bought him a goddamned Christmas tree and ornaments and lights that half worked.

His lips twitched, thinking about her arguing and bribing that little old lady in the store, just so he could have Charlie Brown's tree in his house. Her words, her description, but it was the best tree he'd ever had.

Truthfully.

No bullshit.

She'd given him something he hadn't even known he wanted.

He hadn't bothered decorating for Christmas when his mom had flaked. What was the point of cleaning pine needles off his carpet if he was going to spend his days off playing *Call of Duty* on his couch and eating whatever DoorDash delivered.

But Lily had brought the tree. And ornaments. And lights. And presents—even though he was currently sweltering in his.

And the way she'd looked at him when he'd suggested he make popcorn and hot chocolate to eat and drink during the movie—even though they'd both consumed their body weights in sugar just a few hours earlier at the Pie Extravaganza—had made him feel like he had Hemsworth level superhero skills, even though it was just powdered hot cocoa mix and a couple of bags of microwave popcorn.

She'd popped the DVD in the Xbox, working the control like a pro to get the disc queued up when he'd come back in with the mugs and bowl, having already changed into her pajamas, and by the time he'd crammed his body into *his* onesie and gone back to the living room, she'd downed a large chunk of the popcorn.

Something he'd teased her about.

Something he'd joined her in—even though they'd both eaten

so much at the Pie Extravaganza that it seemed like they couldn't possibly eat more.

Now only...dredges and unpopped kernels remained.

He grinned.

Clearly, they had major carb eating and drinking abilities.

Either that or the movie had him so transfixed that his stomach had reached heretofore unseen proportions.

Either *that* or he was feeding his addiction of Lily.

Speaking of whom, she shifted, curling away from him, tucking her legs beneath her body and pillowing her hands beneath her face.

The cool air soaking in through the onesie was welcome.

The distance wasn't.

And he was only allowing himself to think about that because it was the middle of the night, and she was asleep and...she'd brought him Christmas.

Quietly, he pushed up from the couch, snagged the bowl and mugs, and softly padded into the kitchen. Probably unnecessary considering the shootout with Hans Gruber's men, but he didn't want to wake her.

Which was why he set the dishes in the sink and moved down the hall to the guest bedroom that would now always be Lily's in his mind.

Through the door he'd kept closed over the last weeks.

To the bed he'd definitely avoided.

Snagging the comforter from the top of it.

He settled it over Lily, and then for reasons he wasn't thinking about because it was the middle of the night and now officially Christmas Eve—and people did weird shit on Christmas Eve—he sat next to her, pulled her legs into his lap, and watched the greatest Christmas movie of all time, *Die Hard.*

———

A hand pushing lightly on his chest had his eyes flying open, his body instantly aware.

Of the woman pressed tits to ankles to him.

"Shit," she whispered, the curse barely audible as the blanket slid off their bodies, dropping to the floor. She reached out for it and his arms tightened without thinking, catching her before she toppled off him, keeping them together.

Unable to let her go.

She gasped, eyes shooting down to his.

"Will," she whispered when she realized he was awake.

His dick was hard.

She was on top of him.

He wanted to flip her, to pin her to the couch, unzip that onesie and strip her naked.

Her eyes went wide, like he'd said that aloud, like she'd seen the need raging through him in his eyes and—

She tried to push off him. "I-I'm sorry—"

His hands tightened.

She froze. "Will," she whispered again.

God, she felt good on top of him. Like she belonged there. Like she could live there forever—him, her, his cock, her cunt—

Her. *Cunt*.

Lily's tight, wet pussy convulsing around him.

Lily calling out his name.

Lily who he was supposed to protect—

Bile burned the back of his throat, and he unlocked his arms.

She rolled off him, toppled to the floor, narrowly missing the corner of the coffee table.

"Fuck. Lil!" He sat up. "Shit, I'm sorry, I—"

She pushed her bangs off her face as she sat back on her knees. "I'm sorry," she said quietly. "I don't know what happened. I—"

Teeth in a plump pink lip.

He wanted *his* teeth in it. He wanted...her.

Period.

Just that simple.

And he knew that he had a choice here.

He could push her away, could enact asshole, could fuck things up, could—

Stop staring at her and table the conflicting feelings and just be in this moment with her.

"We fell asleep," he said, sliding from the couch and kneeling in front of her, taking her arms in his hands and helping her to her feet. "That's all. No big deal, right?"

She'd frozen when he touched her, but his words sent something across her face, there and gone before he could discern it, there and gone before he could say anything else.

"Right," she murmured. "No big deal."

"Now," he said, knowing the moment to push on that front had passed, "how are we going to make more Christmas traditions?"

For a second, her brows drew together.

Then her expression cleared, and he could almost see the light bulb flash to life over her head.

Ding.

She had an idea.

Thank fuck for that because he was fresh out of them.

"Is your stomach recovered sufficiently from our bingeing last night for more junk food?"

"Rebecca gave us a whole week of Cheat Days," was his reply.

"Okay then," she said, smiling. "Get ready for the best day of your life."

TWENTY

LILY

He groaned, rubbed his stomach, and sat back on the couch. "You're a bad influence."

She rubbed her hands together, evil genius style. "You're the one who said you had a Cheat Week instead of a Cheat Day." She burped, which was...well, it wasn't sexy, but considering they were apparently making their best effort to play the lead roles in a buddy comedy, she wasn't embarrassed.

Not *too* much anyway.

His lips tipped up when she excused herself, but he didn't comment further on her poor manners.

She picked up the remote. "*Home Alone* or *Love Actually*?"

His eyes slid open. "Is that a real question?"

"*Home Alone* it is then."

That mouth curved again, and she couldn't help but stare at it for a heartbeat too long. Again. Because he had a tiny scar crossing his bottom lip.

And she wanted to kiss it.

And he was—

"Lil?"

She blinked. "Yeah?"

"You don't have to keep hanging out with me, you know? I'm fine, and you've put your time in and—"

Her brows shot up, and she set the remote down. "You think this is a pity hang?"

"Well, I certainly don't think you'd be sitting on my couch snarfing junk food if you hadn't heard my mom wasn't coming."

Yeah, she probably wouldn't be, even with the white lie to her own mom.

But that wasn't why she'd come.

It was...the way he'd been himself but not. It was the Shirley Temple. It was his expression at the Pie Extravaganza.

Will wasn't right.

She...wanted to help him get straightened out.

Plus, that was her job, right?

Get the guys' heads sorted so they could focus on hockey.

Will needed that.

Will needed her.

Will needed—

Hell. She couldn't lie. *She* needed it too, needed some justification that he was the Will she'd remembered, the Will her parents still raved about, the Will she'd written about in her diary. If he'd changed, if he'd become a controlling a-hole who bore no resemblance...

Well, it would hurt.

It shouldn't matter, not to her life, not to her job, not to her future.

Except...it did.

Because *he* mattered.

"So," he said, making her realize that she was staring again, staring when she should really be assuring him that she was here because she wanted to be.

And *that* was the truth.

And *that* was dangerous.

Because she wanted to be there and she needed to be in his house, lounging in a onesie, stuffing her face.

Because...she needed to be with Will.

"So," he said again. "This is me letting you off the hook. Go home—go to that secret apartment of yours, the address of which I'll pretend I didn't get from your parents"—her brows dragged together, and he lifted his head up, eyes dancing—"by pretending I'd lost it and needed to drop something by."

She opened her mouth.

"Sleep in your own bed, and I can take you out to eat tomorrow."

"On Christmas?" she asked incredulously.

"We'll have Chinese or something." A shrug of one big, broad shoulder. "This is me letting you off the hook, sweetheart."

The *sweetheart* had her pulse speeding up, but she managed to think beyond that, to focus on what he'd said and not the pitter-patter in her belly the endearment invoked.

"Have I given you any indication that I want to be let off the hook?" she asked softly.

His lips pressed flat.

"No," she answered since he seemed determined not to. "I haven't. Because it's fun spending time with you and because I don't want to be alone for Christmas—"

"Which begs the question of why you're alone in the first place," he said quietly.

She sucked in a breath. He wasn't supposed to have noticed that fact, wasn't supposed to notice that her not going home for the holiday was anything.

Because it was something.

And...

She exhaled. "My parents heard about the trial"—hell, everyone had; it had been a top news story for weeks—"and they..."

"What?"

"You saw me," she whispered. "I pulled it together"—slightly —"by the time I talked to them, but they knew it hit me hard—"

"Of course it did."

She bit her lip then exhaled, blowing out the noxious fumes that settled in her belly every time she thought about Zack, about what he'd done, about what the fucking organization had condoned in response.

"Yeah," she whispered. "So they've been checking in and wanting to come out and—" She broke off, shook her head.

"You needed some space to wrap your head around it."

Lil blew out a breath. "Yeah. And you know how they are."

"They love you."

Another nod. "Yes, but sometimes their concern makes it hard to breathe."

"You need space."

She shrugged. "Space is helpful."

"And a guy ordering you a Shirley Temple isn't that?"

Laughter in her belly. "Are you actually making a joke about Shirley Temples?"

He leaned forward and tugged lightly at the end of her ponytail. "Well, Shirley seems destined to stay, so I think the only way to survive is to accept it and then laugh about it."

"That's very healthy."

A shake of his head. "Either that or they've fully broken me."

Her lips curved. "I shouldn't laugh at that."

"Except you're going to."

She giggled. "Yup. But know I'm not laughing from a professional perspective. It's purely..."

"Evil?"

"Rude." She narrowed her eyes. "But also probably true."

He grinned, tugged her ponytail again. "I'm just saying, sweetheart, if you want to escape, the time is nigh."

She didn't bother to dignify that with a response. Just picked up the remote and started to point it at the TV. "It's Christmas"

—she nodded to the clock sitting above the TV, which had just ticked over to midnight—"so shut up, sit back, and get ready to enjoy the creative debauchery of the youngest McCallister—"

"It's Christmas?" His gaze flicked to the clock then back to hers.

"That's what I said." She started to press the button. "And no trying to get out of it, I'm staying through presie time—" She looked over her shoulder. "And *that's* not a request for a present. I've sprung my presence on you and taken over your TV for more than twenty-four hours. I'll whip up some omelets—because we need something that isn't refined sugar and it's the only thing I can cook—and let you open the absolutely *epic* gift I got you. Then I'll go home to my apartment and if you're not desperately sick of me, I'll let you bring me takeout for dinner."

He stood up, walked out of the room.

And...okay, she hadn't thought her offer of omelets was *that* bad.

"Um," she called. "I mean...I can really go, Will. If you're sick—"

He strode back into the room, a gaily wrapped box in his hands.

"—of me, I can leave—"

The package landed in her lap, and she felt her lips fall open. "I—"

"If we're doing Christmas, I'm not waiting until the sun is up for presie time." He nudged it closer. "Open your present, sweetheart."

Sweetheart.

"But," she whispered, "how did you—"

Fingers on her chin, tilting it up so that he could meet her eyes. "Open it."

Her pulse had sped up at the *sweetheart*. His quiet order made it beat even faster, so much so that her breaths had shortened, increased in repetition, her throat had gone dry, her mind was starting to spin.

But, for once, she didn't argue with him about the order.

She just slid a finger under the edge of the wrapping paper and tore open the present.

TWENTY-ONE

She froze.

Just went utterly, totally still, and fuck, he'd screwed up again, presumed to know her when a decade had passed, when he didn't, *couldn't*.

"It's nothing, sweetheart," he murmured. "I just happened to see it and thought of you. I'll get you something better, I promise—"

Her head shot up, almost cracking him in the chin, it moved so fast, hands closing over his when he would have taken the box back. "It's *not* nothing," she snapped, tugging it out of his grip, holding it close to her chest. "This is— *Will.*"

Her voice broke and he realized that her eyes were glassy.

Shit.

"Lil, honey, I—"

She swallowed. "It's not nothing," she whispered, gently touching a finger to the contents of the box.

Items that had reminded him of her.

Items he'd bought because Christmas was coming and even

though he'd significantly messed up, he knew she would like them, that they would make her smile.

Except…she was going to cry.

He saw it in her eyes, saw it in the way they glimmered and shone, turning the irises into glittering gemstones. He saw it in the slight wobble of her bottom lip and the way her hands shook.

"I—" She clamped her mouth closed, shook her head slightly.

"Sweetheart," he whispered.

A deep breath in. A long, steady exhale out. Then she lifted her head, eyes going to his. "Thank you."

Two words that gave him those superhero vibes again.

"Lil."

She touched his cheek. Lightly. But her fingertips burned through his beard, seared into his skin, rocketed through his blood, sending his heart thudding against his ribs. "Thank you," she whispered again.

"You're welcome," he whispered back.

Their faces were close. Their breaths intermingling. The heat from her fingers scorching, but he could also feel the warmth of her body, smell the soft, sweet scent of her.

And—fuck—he wanted to taste those lips, to touch every inch of that body, to press his palm to her chest and feel her heart pound against his skin.

His cock twitched.

His throat tightened.

His fingers clenched into taut fists.

Need was a blazing inferno in his nerves, his mind, in every cell.

She leaned closer. He inched nearer.

Their mouths had aligned, mere millimeters separating their lips. He only had to lean in, to close that last little bit of distance between them.

He couldn't stop himself.

He had to taste her.

He shifted—

The opening notes of Christmas music blared through the room, chattering about packing quickly following suit.

Lily jerked back, nearly upending the package before she steadied it.

Another inhale, exhale, the pink tip of her tongue flicking out, tracing the edges of that lush mouth.

Fuck.

As though she heard that curse ricocheting about his mind, she froze, eyes wide, a deer going still in a pair of bright headlights.

He brushed his knuckles over her cheek, hating that she jumped again.

"Popcorn?" he asked softly.

She bit her lip, eyes drifting away from his, over his shoulder, presumably to the TV, staying there for a long moment.

Then they came back.

"Yeah," she whispered. "And I could go for some hot chocolate."

Disappointment through his middle, but he pushed it down, knew it was fucking dangerous ground he was tap dancing over. Landmines. Hidden crevices. Sharp spikes and flesh-eating bacteria and—

He pushed up, taking the box from her lap and setting it gently on the coffee table. "You start the movie over," he told her. "I'll rustle up the junk food."

A ghost of a smile as she reached for the remote.

He smiled back, started for the kitchen.

"Will?"

Feet sliding to a stop, he glanced over his shoulder, eyes flicking to hers. "Yeah, sweetheart?" he asked, knowing he shouldn't call her that, knowing it crossed lines, but not caring.

"You didn't get to open your present."

This woman had brought him Christmas, had made this holiday his best ever—better even than the ones he'd spent with her family (though never Christmas, he'd always flown home for Christmas because his mom pretended then, pretended she wanted him there, even if she'd ignored him the entire time)—and she was worried about him having the chance to open a present.

"I'll open it over omelets, yeah?"

Teeth in her bottom lip. Then she nodded, mouth curving up. "Deal."

The movie paused; he made his way into the kitchen.

Popcorn was popped. Hot chocolate powder mixed with milk and heated. Extra marshmallows plunked into her mug just because she liked them.

Then he was back on the couch, eating too much, and watching a nine-year-old wreak havoc on some burglars.

And when Lily's weight hit his side, he didn't resist wrapping his arms around her.

He just held her close and let his heavy lids slide closed.

———

The phone rang.

And rang.

And...rang.

And...rang.

And...voicemail.

"Christ," he muttered, dropping his cell on the counter, hearing the tin-like quality of his mom's voice telling him to leave a message.

That she wouldn't return.

Even though it was Christmas.

His stomach started to churn, old emotions he worked hard to keep buried began to rise up in his torso, his mind.

Mostly questions that began with why.

Why him?

Why didn't she want to spend time with him?

Why didn't she *love* him?

Why—

A flash catching the corner of his eye, drawing his gaze to the living room, to the half-lit lights on the tree. To the small trash bag of discarded wrapping paper on the floor next to the front door. To the dishes in the sink, mostly consisting of popcorn and hot cocoa remains.

The beep from his phone's speaker caught his focus and he reached out, hit the button to end the call.

Lily had gone back to her place for "real clothes" and to order them a dinner that she'd promised "has marginally more nutritional quality than popcorn and hot chocolate."

This wasn't necessarily something he was looking forward to.

Not the ordering in of the more nutrient-dense food, or even putting on "real clothes."

But breaking the spell that had meant Lily left his house.

He'd woken hard and holding her close that morning, only gently shifting her off him when nature had called—no, *demanded.*

By the time he'd come out of the bedroom, she'd gone to the kitchen and his present had been sitting on the counter—it was a sweater that was nice enough he could wear it by itself or under a jacket to games and soft enough that he'd wanted to stroke it— and then stroke her skin to see which was softer.

Omelets and the goodbyes.

And...spell broken.

Mostly because he'd let the real world intrude and these feelings, the Why Questions, his call going to voicemail...

Reality.

"Fuck," he muttered, knowing that reality was telling him about more than just his mom's phone habits. It was telling him to back off now, to call Lil and lie, say he was actually tired and couldn't go over. Cut the tie now and still keep things civil.

Friendly.

Them.

The fuckery of that was...he didn't want to.

End things. Cut ties. Keep it just friendly.

He was the sponge, and she was the liquid. He wanted to soak up every last drop of her, wanted to possess and own and learn every inch of her body, every hidden recess of her mind.

He wanted—

His phone buzzed and, for one second, his heart leaped, thinking it was his mom.

Spoiler alert, it wasn't.

But it *was* the universe telling him something.

Because Lily had sent the text.

And for just one more day, he kept the worries and thoughts at bay...and changed into "real clothes."

And drove over to Lily's.

And ate something that was way more nutritious than popcorn and hot chocolate.

Though not quite as nostalgic.

Twenty-Two

The knock at her door had her looking up in surprise.

She was at the practice facility, and it was the day after Christmas. There was an optional on-ice session for the team, but the parking lot had been more than a little sparse when she'd come in.

And Will's car hadn't been in the lot.

Not a surprise. Starting tomorrow, they had three away games the next four nights, and she was sure he had things to do—like packing or laundry or...whatever these guys did to get ready before they went out of town.

Playing *Call of Duty?*

Organizing his underwear drawer?

Beers and bitches?

The first was most likely. The middle made her smile. The last one had her stomach churning, and it wasn't because he might be drinking beer.

She'd woken sprawled on his chest two mornings in a row... and it had felt right.

Like her fantasies come to life.

But the spell had broken. He'd come to dinner on Christmas, left after she'd conned him into watching *Love Actually*, and she hadn't spoken to him since.

So, yeah, she couldn't lie, Brit wasn't the hockey player she wanted knocking on her door.

"Why am I not surprised to see you here?" Brit asked dryly, tapping her finger to her bottom lip. "Working," she added with a hint of disapproval.

Lily folded her hands over each other. "You say that like it's a bad thing."

Brit just shrugged and crossed one ankle over the other, leaning back against the doorframe.

"And like you haven't just gotten off the ice yourself." Lily's mouth tipped up. "*Working.*"

Brit grinned and, God, how the woman still had all her teeth was a feat in itself, especially for a hockey player. But that perfect smile was something else. It had graced billboards, been featured in online ads, but seeing it in person...

Warm.

It filled Lily with warmth.

"Takes a workaholic to know one," Brit countered, that smile widening, that warmth growing.

"I will neither confirm nor deny your assumption," Lil said tartly, saving the file she was working on—some team-building strategies she was going to roll out for a certain subset of players who weren't *not* getting along, but who also seemed to be giving each other a deliberate (and wide) berth. "But we both know that's a confirmation in and of itself."

Laughter. "Damn right it is."

She pushed out of her chair, rounded her desk. "What can I help you with?"

"Dinner."

"Going out to dinner?"

A shrug. "We *could* cook if you prefer."

Lily winced. "I'm not the best cook," she warned. "I tend to get creative with recipes and that has a twentyish percent success rate."

"Twenty isn't zero," Brit quipped.

She giggled. "That's true."

"Anyway, I'm not here to discuss your chefly talents—or lack thereof. I just wanted to invite you to join the female contingent for trash television and cocktail night."

Her excitement perked up. "Trash TV?"

Brit shrugged and named Lily's favorite binge of the moment. "It's an addiction and we're all behind."

"I'm only on episode four," she admitted.

"Well, if you don't mind rewatching a couple of episodes. We're going to start at the beginning and go for as long as our bodies and minds can handle the drama."

That sounded really fun. In fact, it sounded much more fun than sitting in her office working her ass off so she didn't focus on the fact that her attorney had finally replied to her email about Zack and company—and it wasn't good news.

The charges had been completely dropped. The prosecutors weren't going to move forward.

Because they couldn't get the girls to testify.

Christ.

Lily had offered to step out of the shadows, to testify, even though it would open her up to public scrutiny and possible personal liability, but without the other testimonies, the case just wasn't strong enough.

It wasn't enough. *She* wasn't enough.

She'd have to settle for winning in the court of public opinion.

That was from her attorney. Verbatim.

Except, while the court of public opinion was harsh and judging, Zack still had a job and was still working with young women and...nothing had really changed.

So, trash TV sounded good.

Trash TV and junk food sounded better.

Trash TV and some girl talk even more so.

She smiled, decided to pounce on the distraction. "I'm down for some mind-melting TV."

Brit fist-pumped. "Yes! We're meeting at my place in an hour. That work for you?"

"I'll see you there."

———

She was jabbing away on her phone screen as she left the practice facility a little while later, ordering some giant, delicious, *addicting* cookies to Brit's place, because even though the other woman had said Lil didn't need to bring anything, Lily wasn't going to show up empty-handed.

Hell, her mom would probably get some sign from the universe that Lil was committing a horrible manners faux pas and she'd get a phone call and—

Lil ordered cookies to prevent disapproving phone calls.

And maybe also because the cookies were delicious and addicting.

Grinning, she started toward her car, but a shadow had her rocking back on her heels, her heart in her throat. "I—" She clamped a hand to her chest when the shadow materialized into a woman. "Can I help you?"

"Sorry," the other woman whispered, backing up, her hands extended, palms out. "I wasn't trying to scare you. I—" She bit her lip, deep brown eyes growing worried. "I just finished watching practice and was putting directions into my phone. I wasn't trying to start any trouble. I promise."

Okaaay. Right.

This was pushing her spidey sense well beyond her normal already-heightened status.

She looked closer at the other woman. "Did you need some help?"

Wide brown eyes. A sharp shake of her head. "N-no," she said quickly. "Don't let me keep you, I'll just—oh! Look"—she held up her phone, screen out—"it's working now and—"

Lil moved a little closer. "Do you need to talk to someone? I'm a good listener."

"No." Softer now. "I—" She cleared her throat. "Really, I just came to watch my brother. And then my phone really wasn't loading directions. I'm not trying to start trouble." She swallowed and it looked painful, even from a few feet away. "For *once*, I'm not trying to start trouble. I just...needed to see he was really okay, I guess."

Lily exhaled softly. "Your brother."

A nod. "Ben."

Oh. *Oh.*

Oh *shit*.

This was Ben's sister. The former addict—or, she supposed, current one, since addiction wasn't something that was just went away, rehab or not. But anyway, this was Ben's sister who had a boatload of trauma that had bled over into Ben's life...

Up until just a few months before.

Shit.

"I see you've heard of me."

Yeah. Lily had.

And very little of it was good.

"I'm just heading home," Ben's sister said, backing up a step. "I just—"

"I'm Lily," she blurted, sticking out her hand.

Hesitation before soft fingers wrapped around Lily's. "Maddy."

"Nice to meet you, Maddy." She leaned back against her car. "So how'd your brother do at practice?"

More hesitation, but Lily felt the tension release from Maddy's body, saw the edges of her lips curve up. "He could move his feet a bit more."

Lily chuckled. "I've heard Calle"—one of the team's coaches —"say that once or twice."

"I bet." Maddy nibbled at her bottom lip. "Well, I should head out. I...um...have a meeting I need to get to."

A meeting.

That was good.

Or maybe, lip service?

Except, Lily's bullshit detector was quiet—very quiet—and, well, she wanted it to be true, so she was going to take it at face value. For the moment.

"Of course." She smiled, extended her hand again. "It was nice to meet you, Maddy. I hope to see you around."

"Yeah. I..." A shake of her head as Maddy grasped her hand.

Then she was stepping back, turning away.

And then...she was gone.

TWENTY-THREE

WILL

He had bags in both hands, one funneling scorching hot steam up his arm, the other surprisingly heavy, considering it was filled mostly with crap.

Making a herculean effort that had his forearm screaming, he lifted the arm with the bag of crap and pressed the doorbell.

Footsteps.

A pause that settled him, that didn't eat away at his insides.

Because it was long enough before the lock clicked and the door started to open that she had time to check the peephole, but not so long it appeared she was trying to avoid him.

Then the door was all the way open, and Lily was standing in front of him.

Gorgeous without a stitch of makeup on.

Body sexy as fuck even though she was in sweats and a T-shirt.

Smile genuine and totally fucking kissable.

He shouldn't be here, shouldn't be risking the temptation of this, of *her*, but he'd started ignoring that voice in his head a week ago and he hadn't seen her since Christmas Day and...

He'd missed her.

So...he'd gotten back from the road game, had slept off the jet lag, done some shopping.

Now he was here.

On her doorstep.

"Will," she said, her voice a warm balm down his spine, "what are you doing here?"

He did another herculean lift of the bags. "I'm bringing you New Year's Eve."

Her brows dragged together, lips parting on an inhale. "You're bringing me New Year's Eve?" she asked quietly.

"Yeah." A beat, his stomach sinking when her face didn't change. "You got plans?"

"Yeah," she replied softly. "I've got plans."

Fuck.

He hadn't considered *that* being part of this evening's endeavors. "Oh," he began. "I...um..."

"With you," she said lips curving up, gripping his arm when he would have turned away, and tugging the bag of food off his wrist, saving him from third-degree burns. "Come in, Shirley. My Xbox is on, and I was trying to decide which game I was going to crush you in."

"You're hilarious," he said dryly, even though his belly had filled with warmth.

Because...his pixie and her giant heart.

"Yes, I am," she said lightly, marching across the room and setting the bag of food on the coffee table. "Now, pop off those shoes, get comfy, and grab a remote. I'll get the beers."

"Wine would go better with the pasta I picked up."

She slowed, spun back to face him.

His lips twitched. "You tolerate beer," he pointed out. "You *love* wine."

"This much is true." She started walking again. "Red?"

"Is it your favorite?" he countered.

Another stutter step, but she didn't look back this time, just continued into the kitchen, her soft "Yes," barely reaching his ears.

He unpacked the bag of food and was snagging the second controller when she came back into the room with two filled wine glasses and the bottle of red tucked beneath one arm. "So we don't have to go far for refills."

Fuck.

This was a woman a man could love.

Especially when she gave him that soft look again as she glanced inside the containers and saw the chicken parmesan, as though he'd won the lottery just because he remembered her favorite Italian dish. Or maybe that was because he'd brought chocolate cake.

And champagne.

The latter of which he put in the fridge to chill.

The cake, though, didn't make it past the first round of *Call of Duty*. And they'd gotten into the champagne before they turned off the game a couple of hours later, well before they'd tuned into the New Year's Eve special.

Considering that was *after* polishing off the bottle of red (along with another cabernet Lil had been gifted for Christmas), they were more than a little tipsy as the pop princess with the killer voice began singing on the screen—duets and solos and introductions of artists Will had never heard of. And maybe it was the wine that had softened his critique skills, or maybe he'd been stuck in his musical lane too long, or perhaps, more likely, he'd been subliminally affected by Brit's pop music obsession when it was her turn to control the playlist in the locker room. Regardless, he was bopping his head and enjoying the show as time ticked down and they closed in on midnight.

The new year was only minutes away when Lil turned to him and asked a question that threatened to disperse his buzz.

"Is it me or my dad?"

He shifted to face her, careful to not dislodge her feet that had found their way into his lap. Will had ignored their initial appearance, just as he'd ignored how his hands had moved to them, how his fingers had begun to massage the soles.

Needing to touch her.

Needing to keep her close.

"What do you mean, sweetheart?"

Pink cheeks. He didn't know if it was the wine and the champagne or the query itself, though he had his suspicions when she said the next, "You know exactly what I mean."

"It's not you," he said quickly.

"So, it's my dad. Did—" Those cheeks grew pinker. "Did he advise you against me or—"

"No." His fingers tightened on her feet and he had to consciously loosen his grip. "Your dad wouldn't do that, sweetheart. He loves you."

"And he loves you, too," she whispered. "You're like another son to him, and I'm...well, my life has been a bit of a mess and I wouldn't blame him, or you, if he told you to avoid the dumpster fire that was my life lately and—"

Now he shoved her feet from his lap, but it wasn't to create distance.

It was to move their bodies closer.

Because he couldn't believe what he was hearing.

"Please tell me that you're not saying what I think you're saying," he whispered.

She huffed out a breath. "My life is a disaster. I work too much. I can't cook to save my life. I watch crap TV and drink too much wine and am way too addicted to fluffy pancakes."

"Sweetheart—"

"And I got fired because I stole confidential documents. And I couldn't protect my girls. And"—she released a shaky breath—"I'm only here because Charlotte has a soft spot for people who try to do the right thing, not necessarily because the team needs me—"

"Right," he said, deliberately cutting her off. "So all of that is bullshit." He shrugged when her expression turned outraged.

"Okay, not *all* of that—you do watch crappy shows and work too much. But the rest of it is nonsense."

Her eyes narrowed. "Will—"

"First of all, wine and fluffy pancakes are the shit. And Char is a smart, successful GM because she has a heart, but she's not a pushover, and fuck with her, fuck with the team, and you're going down. The reason you're here is because she saw there was a spot for you. She saw that you would bring value to the organization." He leaned forward, cupped her jaw. "We're family, yes, but the team is also a business and Char is accountable for all of us. There isn't dead weight. There isn't bringing someone on just because they're nice and she feels bad for them."

"But—"

"As for the rest of it, you stood up, you said something, you tried to help them." He bent closer, until he could see the gold flecks hidden amongst the green and brown of her eyes. "You didn't fail them, sweetheart."

Her lids slid closed, shutting him out of the turmoil happening in her mind.

But he could see it in her face, in the lines on either side of her mouth, in the creases at the corners of her eyes, the frown lines between her brows.

So, he kept talking. "And I don't give a fuck that you can't cook or what shows you watch. I think you're awesome, sweetheart."

Her lids peeled open. "You say that," she whispered. "You say that, and you call me *sweetheart* and I feel that in my belly, in my heart"—those cheeks went pink again and her throat worked— "in my pussy."

His inhalation was sharp. "Lil."

"Yeah," she said, still whispering. "That's the problem."

Twenty-Four

She'd opened a can of worms.

But...the man had split her wide open—heart to mind to the butterflies fluttering in her stomach.

The music faded, voices she couldn't be bothered to decipher increasing in volume.

"Yeah," she whispered, "that's the problem."

Because she'd talked about her attraction, said something a little bit dirty, and...he'd pulled back.

"Your dad."

A blade *snicking* home, sliding between her ribs. She looked away at the screen, the camera lens having focused on the large glittering ball.

Ready to drop.

But her heart already had.

"Ten!" the voices yelled on the TV.

"And your brother."

Her heart sank further, dropping like that ball.

"And your mother."

"Nine!"

She bit the inside of her mouth.

"And you."

Her gaze shot back to his.

"Eight!"

"Because I want you so fucking bad."

Her pulse sped.

"Seven!"

"And I don't care if it complicates everything."

She sucked in a breath.

"Six!"

"And I don't care if your family thinks I'm a shitty match for you."

Lil's brows drew together.

"Five!"

"And I almost don't care if you think that too."

Her lips parted.

"Four!"

"Because I don't care any longer that I'm not worthy of you."

More butterflies. Her breathing increasing in speed.

"Three!"

"I don't care that it's better for you if I stay away."

His fingers flexed on her cheek, drawing their mouths even closer.

"Two!"

"I want you, sweetheart," he rasped, the words hot puffs on her lips. "And I'm going to have you."

She started to say something—who the fuck knew what—but then his mouth was on hers.

"One!"

"Auld Lang Syne" began playing in the background, but she barely heard it, barely heard the shouts of "Happy New Year!" She didn't fully process the cheers or that it was a new year, a fresh start.

Because Will's mouth was on hers.

Because his tongue was sliding between her lips and he was

sitting back, drawing her onto his lap, encouraging her to straddle him.

Hard.

His chest, his stomach, the granite-like erection pressing between her thighs.

He groaned, wrapped his arm around her middle, one hand on her jaw, tilting her head so that his tongue could delve deeper, so he could kiss her until she was lost in the moment, lost in *him*.

Roughened fingertips on her jaw, drifting down her throat, diving into her hair, pulling lightly, pulling until a slight sting on her scalp had moisture pooling between her thighs, had her hips bucking, grinding against the hard length of his cock.

And *God*, that was good.

God, that had her wanting more.

The layers between them disappeared. The stretch and pull and fullness of him sliding into her. Fingers on her nipples, pinching hard, sending lightning bolts of pleasure through her belly, into her pussy.

A nip to her bottom lip. "Pay attention," he ordered.

"I—"

Another nip. Another kiss—deeper and hotter and longer than before. "I *said* pay attention."

And *God*, his orders...yeah, she hated them out in the real world, but here, in Sex Land, in Orgasm Imminent Island with his big body bucking beneath hers, flipping them effortlessly so she was on her back on the couch, all the glorious heat and hardness of him pressing her down into the cushions, they were some of the best things she'd ever experienced.

Of course, she hadn't had his cock thrusting deep.

Not yet.

She knew in her belly *that* would be transcendental.

He pushed off her, and for one horrible moment, she thought he was going to stop, to withdraw, to pull away, but then he was reaching for the waistband of her sweats, tugging them down her thighs, exposing her legs to the cool of the midnight air.

He left her socks on her feet, but drew off her taco-emblazoned underwear, cursing softly under his breath when she parted her legs.

One hot fingertip trailing up the inside of her leg, passing just barely over the damp heat of her pussy, making her gasp and arch, seeking more pressure, for more of that finger.

For it to slip inside and thrust deep.

Instead, though, he trailed it down her other thigh, along the inside of her knee, to her ankle.

Off went her sock. Then the other.

Then he was bending and pressing a kiss to her calf, her knee, her upper thigh.

A flick of his tongue along her labia that had her gasping.

Suction that had her eyes rolling back.

Then he was reaching for the hem of her sweatshirt, tugging it along with her tank top over her head. And freezing.

"Fuck!" he growled.

Her vision had hazed. Her body was on fire.

"What?" she asked blearily.

"If I'd known you weren't wearing a fucking bra, Lil, I would have done this hours ago."

"Hindsight"—she gasped when he bent, sucked one of her nipples deep—"is"—another gasp when he sucked at the other—"twenty-twenty."

His mouth was on her throat, her jaw, dragged down to her collarbones, tasting one and then the other before moving in a flurry of lips and teeth and tongue down to her breasts. He wasn't gentle. He was big and rough and in a frenzy.

But she was right there with him.

Gripping his hair, dragging him back to her nipples when he would have moved farther down her body, hips bucking, legs wrapping around his waist.

Grinding.

Moaning.

Arching.

Then he'd had enough, breaking free of her hold, moving down her torso and burying his face between her thighs, showing that same amount of rough and frenzied only this time on her pussy, sucking at her clit, tonguing her opening, nibbling and licking and kissing her.

"Will!" she gasped, head pressing into the cushions, back arching, legs having gone tight around his shoulders.

He growled, nipped her a little harder.

She bucked, her orgasm barreling down on her. She just needed—

One long, thick finger slid up the crease of her ass, pressed into her pussy.

"Fuck," he groaned against her. "This tight, wet cunt is going to clench me so fucking good."

She gasped.

He stroked deeper, mouth going back to work, tongue and teeth driving her up the edge—

Over the edge.

Her cry burst free from her mouth, loud and piercing and long enough that her voice gave out. Or maybe that was her body, slumping against the cushions as he worked her, wave after wave of pleasure coursing through her.

"Will," she whispered when he flicked his tongue over her clit, sending her jerking, the pleasure almost too much.

He did it again.

"*Will.*"

Another finger joined the one still inside her, circling and stretching her and—

"*Will!*"

He grinned up at her, beard dripping, teeth flashing, and slowly slid his fingers from her.

"Inside, honey," she whispered.

And, thank God, he didn't hesitate, didn't question, didn't retreat.

Not when she reached for his shirt and yanked it over his head. Not when she divested him of his jeans and boxer briefs.

He just reached for his jeans and tugged out his wallet, extracting a condom before he tossed the leather billfold onto the table.

Approximately three second later, he was rolling it down the length of his cock, moving back over her, notching the head of his erection at her entrance.

"Will," she whispered.

His eyes—blazing, the blue darkened with need—held hers.

Then he thrust in, and it was still a little rough, still a little frenzied...and more than a little big. Almost too big, almost too much, especially when he bottomed out, his pelvis hitting hers for long enough that they both groaned. But that was only for a second.

Because then he was retreating, pulling back.

Thrusting in.

Out. In. *Out. In.*

Until her hands were in his hair again, her nails digging into his scalp, her legs tightening around his waist.

Until pleasure was tightening, spiraling higher, dragging her up the slope, dangerously close to that peak again.

"I—"

He did something with his hips, something that should have been illegal.

Something that shot her right over the edge.

And he was there with her, cock stroking, body pistoning, her name on his lips as he shuddered and groaned and fell apart.

As he...gathered her close and made her think that this—*this* —could keep them both together.

Forever.

TWENTY-FIVE

WILL

They'd made it to a bed this time.

But she was still curled up against him, her breath on his throat, his arms around her.

His stomach in turmoil.

His heart aching and scared and—

She sighed, body arching against his, making his already hard cock harden further, aching as much as his heart.

More.

Masking the urge to run, the storm that was gathering in his belly, swirling rapidly, swelling up and out and filling his insides, his mind with clouds and lightning and thunder.

Because if the storm of desire took over, if it was just need and want and orgasms then—

Lily sighed again, and the damp heat of her breath hit his throat again.

He knew the moment she finally woke up because her body went still, and her breath hitched in and—

Carefully, she pushed up enough to look down at him.

Worry in those hazel eyes, caution in her frame.

"Morning," she murmured.

Fuck.

He couldn't do this.

"Morning," he said back, his tone neutral, but she was smart, she was intuitive. She no doubt could see the turmoil on his face, but her expression didn't change as she pushed up a little further, her mouth curving.

"You're in for a special treat," she murmured. "I have the ingredients to make a meal I've recently mastered"—a grin that had his heart squeezing tight—"and that's mostly because I can throw bacon on a cookie sheet and add water to pancake mix—"

"Lil—"

She slid off him, giving him a glimpse of an ass he hadn't yet had the chance to stroke and pay homage to. Hadn't been able to kiss and bite and, maybe, get inside. Then she'd snagged a pair of pajamas from a drawer in her dresser, had tugged a sweatshirt over her head. "I need to warm up the griddle and"—she crossed back over to him, slanted her mouth over his for a brief kiss that set his heart aching all over again—"locate the chocolate chips."

Chocolate chip pancakes.

Bacon.

He sucked in a breath.

Her dad's—also hopeless in the kitchen—meal, the only one he could cook.

"I woke up this morning," she said softly, pausing with her hand on his chest, resting over his heart, no doubt feeling how the organ was pounding beneath her palm. "I woke up and I was home."

His lungs spasmed, the breath sliding out.

"I woke up and I thought, *this is exactly where I want to be.*" A beat. "Exactly," she whispered, lightly brushing her mouth over his again.

Fuck. *Fuck.*

Her fingers tightened, just enough that her nails bit into his chest, broke him out of the panic gripping his insides.

Then her hand was gone, and she was padding out of the room.

"Take a shower," she called over her shoulder, pausing on the threshold. "Or don't," she added. "Just relax"—a grin as she turned for the hall—"and I'll slave away in the kitchen."

Her smile widened.

She disappeared, leaving his insides filled with that storm.

"Fuck," he whispered.

He couldn't do pancakes—or maybe he *shouldn't*.

Or maybe—

"Fuck," he whispered again, running a hand through his hair and clenching the strands.

He should go.

He should get dressed, get the fuck out, get—

Pans clattered in the kitchen.

Chocolate chip pancakes and bacon.

Not nutritious.

But Cartwright.

He tossed the covers back, going to the bathroom and splashing water on his face, using some mouthwash then snagging a towel and wrapping it around his waist so he wouldn't give her the full Magic Mike experience as he retrieved his clothes from the front room.

The irony—towels and nakedness—didn't pass him by as he moved to the crumpled pile of clothing on the floor, crammed between the table and couch, sifting through it until he found his underwear.

Then his pants.

And shirt.

And socks.

By the time he'd pulled them on, the smell of bacon cooking had hit his nose. And he was no closer to figuring out what the fuck all was going on in his head. Shouldn't and couldn't and get the fuck out. Stop and pause and *think.*

What it would do to her if he pulled this shit.

How her face would change.

The disappointment and hurt and—

"Soup's up!" she called.

Fuck. *Fuck.*

He set her clothes in a folded pile on the couch, next to the towel he'd also folded—not that he was delaying or anything—and moved into the kitchen.

"Do you want syrup with your pancakes?" she asked, eyes on the griddle, focused on turning the hotcakes. The flips complete, she spun to face him. "Or whipped cream on these perfectly crafted chocolate-chip-laced discs of carbs? Which is my preferen..."

Will saw the moment she realized he'd dressed, not just tugging his pants on for propriety's sake, and her face...fuck, it killed him.

Because it changed.

Because the happiness in her eyes faded, the pride from her pancake accomplishment disappearing.

And disappointment flooded him, hitting him hard and deep like a knife to the kidney.

"Or," she whispered, "I can pack them up for you to go."

"Lil—"

"No," she said, voice rising as she spun back toward the cabinets, tugging one of the doors open. "I probably *should* pack them up for you to take home." An exhale. "And bacon too."

"Lily, sweetheart—"

She spun, the spatula clutched in her hand. "Don't, Will," she snapped. "I'm not going to stand here while you convince yourself what we did was something wrong or something you need to punish yourself for or something that you don't deserve." The spatula swung wide as she rotated sharply to face him again. "Pick your poison, but don't try to shove it down my throat. This isn't my issue. It's yours."

She turned back to the open cabinet, began rustling amongst the containers, pulling one out and slamming it on the counter.

The lid followed a second later.

"Sweetheart—"

Another swing of that spatula, nearly smacking him in the face because he'd moved closer, because the plastic container and the lid weren't the only things slamming in the kitchen. Her words into his brain, his heart, the tornado in his stomach, the indecision wracking him with guilt.

Because he wanted her, wanted this—pancakes in the morning, cuddling on the couch at night, someone to hold and laugh with and comfort. Someone who could be his.

His family.

His love.

His life—

"Just go, Will. We'll call this a...holiday fling and move on. Back to friendship and Shirley Temples and focus on work."

The spatula shoved beneath the pancake, scooped it out of the pan.

Dumped it in the container.

And Will got it.

This was the moment.

The puck was sailing up the ice, flying toward his stick as the other team's defense barreled down on him. He could let the pass go through, get an icing call, make his teammates work harder to save his own ass.

Or he could go for that puck, put it all on the fucking line, and help his team, have the play develop into something else.

Something better.

Something fucking *perfect.*

Now or never.

Put up or shut the fuck up. Forever.

And well...he couldn't live without Lily. Not for a few months. Not years. Not forever. Not again.

Not when—

Another pancake hit the container.

He reached forward, flicked off the burner.

And he went for the fucking puck.

TWENTY-SIX

She jumped when his arm brushed her side.

Blinked when the burner turned off.

Jerked when his front pressed to her back.

All the sharp words that she'd been preparing, that had bubbled up in the back of her throat, ready to leap off her tongue, stoppered up, stuck together.

"I'm not leaving," he murmured, wrapping his arms around her.

Her tongue relaxed, those words came—or different ones, anyway. "You were."

A soft laugh in her ear. "Yeah, pixie, I was." His teeth closed lightly over her earlobe, and she shivered. "Call it a moment of insanity. I'm here now."

"Now," she muttered, even though his teeth on her skin had her shivering. "For *now.*"

He straightened enough to spin her around, and her breath caught at the look in his eyes. "I'm here."

Not evasive.

Not avoiding her eyes.

Not with guilt in his.

Instead...there was *need*.

Lily's heart leaped, bouncing against her rib cage like a flopping fish, but her thighs pressed together, heat blooming in her belly, her pussy going slick, moisture coating the tops of her legs. In a freaking *instant*.

One glance of blazing blue irises, and she was molten.

Ready.

"You're here," she whispered.

He nodded, fingers sliding under the hem of her sweatshirt, brushing along her back, skating up her sides, leaving her skin covered with gooseflesh.

"I'm here, pixie. And I'm not going anywhere."

"Will—" She exhaled.

"Just us for now," he whispered, leaning close, resting his forehead against hers. "We'll worry about the rest of the world later."

The rest of the world.

The team.

Her parents.

Her father and brother.

His mother.

He was right. That could wait until later. Today—*now*—they could just be them.

"Just us," she agreed.

A nod. "I'm here," he said again.

"I—"

But then he was moving, stealing her words again. This time when he lifted her up, he turned and set her on the island. "Just us." His fingers gripped the bottom of her sweatshirt, wrapped tight, then tugged it up and over her head.

"Just—"

He latched onto her nipple through the thin material of her tank top, his hand diving beneath her sweats and into her panties, groaning when he came upon the slick heat. "God," he growled, yanking at the neck of her tank, pulling it down until her breast popped free. "This fucking cunt of yours. So sweet. So tight. So *fucking* wet."

Her body was on fire, but his words, rough and rasping, skating over her skin before he drew on her nipple again, sent her even higher.

But she didn't want to just sit back, to accept whatever he was willing to give her.

She wanted to give.

To take.

So as good as it felt to have his mouth on her, his fingers working at her pussy, she slid her fingers into his hair and tugged him off her breast, pushing him back.

"Pixie—"

A nip to his bottom lip.

Another push to his chest—until he got the hint and slid off her, concern growing in his eyes.

She didn't worry about that, though, because she knew it would be a momentary blip.

Another nudge back gave her enough room to slither off the counter...

To slide between his body and the island...

To drop to her knees and work at the button on his jeans.

Yeah, that worry disappeared.

Heat took its place.

She flicked open the button, tugged the tag of the zipper, drawing it down, shoving his jeans off his hips, down his thighs, low enough that she could reach for the waistband of his boxer briefs and drag them down as well.

And it was like the best game ever of Whack-A-Mole.

The underwear went down. The cock sprang up...

Right into her mouth.

Or against it, anyway, kissing her lips with a bead of moisture before she parted them, wrapped her fingers around his shaft and guided his cock into her mouth.

He grunted, hands going to the back of her head, tugging her forward.

But barely.

Lightly, as though he wanted to yank her fully onto his cock, bottoming out at the back of her throat.

She wanted that.

Wanted to give him free rein to fuck her mouth. Just...not today. Today she wanted to make him crazy, make him grow harder and thicker and strain her lips. She wanted to drive him *so* crazy that she unleashed the rough and big on her body.

So she stroked, rough and fast.

So she sucked, deep and hard.

So she licked and used her teeth and kept her lips tight and fought tears as she did her best to suck him as deeply as she could take.

Not enough.

But she'd work on that.

Because the way he growled her name when she hit her limit, when she tightened her grip set fire to her veins. Because she fucking *loved* the way he eventually lost control and ripped her off his cock, leaving it hard and glistening and calling out for her lips and mouth and tongue and...cunt.

Then her sweats were off.

Her underwear was on the floor.

Her tank top was ripped over her head.

And he was on *her*, flipping her, bending her over the counter, the granite a shock of cold against her breasts, her stomach.

Heat on her spine.

A rough, warm hand spreading her thighs.

A thick cock thrusting into her.

"Will!" she cried out.

"I'm here," he growled, hand wrapping around the side and front of her throat, pressing in just enough to send another gush of desire between her legs. "I'm *fucking* here."

"You're here," she whispered. "You're here."

The hand tightened on her throat and his other arm slipped around her middle, dipped down to part her labia, to circle and press against her clit, to—

"Oh fuck," she whispered.

Because he'd slipped a finger inside her, curling it up against her G-spot as his cock stroked deep, the heel of his hand pressing into her clit, and...

"Oh fuck," she whispered again.

Because it was coming.

Because...it was going to burn her to cinders.

Because it was *there.*

His hand on her throat tightened, his finger inside her curled further, his palm pressed harder, and his cock...that grew harder, bigger, stroked deeper.

She convulsed around that thick length, milking him as pleasure flowed through her body, feeling his thrusts falter, his breathing grow jagged, his voice in her ear a rasp as he called out her name, as his own orgasm took him under, as he came inside her.

Hot jets of cum hitting her walls.

His cock jerking.

His hips slowing, stopping with his pelvis pressed to her ass, his cock rock-hard inside her, his finger gently pulsing.

"I'm here," she whispered when her vision cleared, when she was able to focus on something that wasn't just sensation and pleasure and this man fucking her into oblivion. "I'm here, too, honey."

He shifted, pulling out, swinging her up into the circle of his arms.

His expression was so fucking gentle that it nearly sent her to tears, and the way he pressed a soft kiss to her forehead caused her vision to go glassy.

Fucking too sweet.

She was in damned trouble.

Especially when that sweet swung straight past sweet and dipped into wicked.

He started to carry her from the kitchen, but as they passed into the hall, her nose kicked in—and it wasn't to smell the lovely, spicy scent of him.

"The bacon!" she cried.

His mouth curved, but he didn't put her down as he made a detour to the oven, as he turned it off, nor when he went back out into the hall.

In fact, he didn't put her down until he reached the bedroom.

And her back hit the mattress.

Twenty-Seven

"Yeah, yeah!" he called, waiting for Ben to pass the puck, watching as the defenseman from the other team closed in on his teammate.

Ben saw it too, glancing up then over to Will.

A slight shake of his head told Will that his teammate had seen something he missed as they started the breakout from their own zone, and a heartbeat later, he understood what exactly it was that he'd missed and Ben had picked up on.

Lucas streaked between them, a flash of black and gold zigzagging through the neutral zone.

Ben didn't hesitate this time, just chipped the puck up and over the opponent's stick, sending it sailing across the ice.

It wasn't clean or pretty and Will was fairly sure the forward from the other team got a piece of it, but Lucas had good hands—great hands, really—so he corralled the puck on his stick without needing to slow down, without hesitating in the least.

Puck out of the air, onto the blade of his stick.

Carrying it over the blue line.

Will wasn't the fastest or most skilled player on the roster. He was a good skater, though, and liked to think his hockey IQ was high.

Not necessarily Einstein level.

But in the one-thirties at least.

He could see plays developing, could guess where they were going, how they'd change, since the game itself was always shifting and moving.

So maybe less IQ and more psychic.

Like right then.

He was still skating, still hauling his ass across the blue line, trailing Ben and Lucas into the zone, but he felt or saw or *psychicked* the play changing ahead of him.

Could predict the breakdown before it was happening.

As it was happening.

So he positioned himself accordingly—sliding what might be considered out of position, for a few moments, anyway—readying himself.

And *bam*.

There it was.

Two players went to Lucas. Two toward the front of the net, one covering Ben...but not really, not in a great place, positionally speaking. And the one that was supposed to be on Will wasn't tracking him correctly, didn't have his head on a swivel.

Probably, he wasn't anticipating Will not being in position.

But that not going to the net, the not appearing to support Lucas as the puck carrier, meant they all took their eyes and focus off Will.

Which meant he could slip in, could get into a good position.

Could...

Lucas dropped the puck.

The two in front of the net forgot about Ben, or unconsciously shifted over, of who the fuck cared? They moved, an opening cleared, and—

Will shot the puck.

Not at the net.

At Ben.

Who tracked it easily through the air, lifted his stick, and—

Tip.

Ben redirected the puck so that it hit the back of the net.

The arena had that moment of quiet, the collective inhalation of breath as they were trying to see the puck, see if it had really crossed the goal line. Then the red light flashed, the fans processed the puck was in the net, and the roar of celebration was almost deafening.

It hit him in his belly, reverberated through his torso.

By then he was already moving, already skating toward Ben and not being gentle about the celebratory hug.

Because it was overtime.

Because they'd just won.

Two points to their total. One step closer to the playoffs. One step closer to the Cup.

And Ben had made a great fucking tip.

Will punched his friend in the shoulder once more, just to show his appreciation for that tip, then hopped up to his skates, his gaze catching on the cheering fans.

On *one* of the cheering fans—or at least one who was smiling and clapping her hands together and standing next to Ben's grinning mom.

Maddy Roberts was in the stands, going through all the correct motions.

Only, instead of her focus being on her brother...

Her eyes were locked on Lucas.

———

"That was a nice pass, Will," Lucas called over the noise in the locker room, mouth curved, something clutched tight in his hand.

"Don't," Will ordered, preparing to dodge a sock ball...

Which would then become a flurry of sock balls.

Because his teammates had no self-control.

Because they were all in a celebratory mood.

Because—

Lucas launched what he'd been clutching over Ben and Axel, nearly taking off the former's face and earning a glare in the process.

Will caught it instinctively, sending his own glare in Lucas's direction.

One he doubled down on when he saw exactly what Lucas had chucked at him.

"You're a real asshole, you know that, right?"

Rome, on his other side, leaned in. "What the—" Then he seemed to process what Will was holding, something Will deduced mostly because Rome busted up, his laughter joining in with Lucas's—and then Ben and Axel's.

And pretty much the entire room was laughing.

At him.

"You're all assholes," he grumbled, which earned him nothing more than a few grins (along with absolutely no abatement of the laughter). "And you"—he swung out a hand, unfortunately the one that was holding the stuffed pair of cherries (because fuck his life), and narrowed his eyes at Rome. "And you," he said again, "can't even drink, so I don't want to hear it."

A wide grin. "But I *am* old enough for a Shirley Temple."

Will sighed, dropping the cherry plush onto the bench and his head back against the wall. "Never. Going. To. Mafia's. Again."

"Lies," Lucas said. "You'll be there next Cheat Day, just like the rest of us."

Since this was unfortunately the truth, Will didn't bother to reply, just continued getting undressed, glad the nickname hadn't made an appearance while the press was in the room—or Scarlett, who ran their social media.

He couldn't begin to imagine the memes and posts and games he'd have to play if she or they did.

Of course, he also knew the reprieve would only be temporary.

Because...someone would let the name slip and then the social media crew would have a great idea and ask him and he'd say yes because he wouldn't give a damn that it was at his own expense.

Because this team was his family.

His life.

Though, not *all* of it any longer, he thought, mouth turning up.

Because of—

"Lily," Brit blurted.

His eyes flashed open, locked with their goalie's, who was smirking across the room from him, stripped down to her sports bra, her hair up in a ponytail. She was on her knees on the floor, undoing the straps on her leg pads.

Pads that protected her from pucks she willingly put herself in front of.

Pads that he *didn't* wear, even though he blocked plenty of shots (and his defensemen even more), doing it with normal skater gear.

Everyone said goalies were weird.

But at least Brit did her job with extra protection from toes to head.

So, who were the weird ones really?

The idiots who willingly stood between the goalposts or the ones who did it without the big pads?

Food for thought.

"It's Lily," she semi-repeated, trademark grin in place, totally having caught him out. Totally having *caught* the entire attention of the locker room.

Fuck.

"Not sure what you're talking about," he hedged.

That grin widened. "Hmm. Sure you don't." A beat, her gaze flicking around the room and mischief lighting her eyes. "*Shirley.*"

He sighed, thunked his head back against the wall, knowing that there was no hope of the nickname dying now that she'd used it in full view of the locker room. It wasn't just the players and the coaches, but the equipment staff and—one eye slit open at a squee (there was really no other way to describe the sound)—the team's publicist.

"Fuck," he muttered as her face lit with glee and she cut a path in his direction, saying, "I have some ideas."

He glared at Brit, who just shrugged and mouthed, "I knew it."

How she knew it, Will had no clue.

Other than Brit was Brit and she was the conductor of the gossip train.

And she knew things. *All* the things.

He should hate the intrusion, the teasing which was likely to increase thanks to Brit's big mouth.

But he could only be happy.

Because this team was his family.

And he wouldn't take them any other way.

TWENTY-EIGHT

LILY

She'd intended on working in her office, loosely watching the game as it played in the background on the TV mounted in the corner of the room, only glancing away from her computer when the crowd indicated the appropriate times.

Instead, she'd found her way to the tunnel and had spent the last hours watching the game with bated breath at ice level.

They were huge when they were on the rink, their skates giving them extra inches, their pads bulking out their forms.

She'd been riveted.

She'd watched the entire game, all the way through overtime, smiling when Brit had launched herself from the net after Ben had scored the game-winning goal, her helmet on the ice, stick and gloves in the net, skating all the way to the other side of the rink and joining in on the dog pile.

They'd beaten one of their top rivals, the Sierra, a newer expansion team in the league, and it had been a back-and-forth battle that had her—and the rest of the fans in the arena—on edge.

Lil *had* managed to tear her gaze from the play on the ice from time to time, studying the interactions on the bench—who was looking confident and relaxed, who was focused, who was sitting purposely separate, who looked tense or nervous or frustrated...or any combination of those emotions she needed to keep a closer eye on.

Notes had been taken—on her phone and in her mind—but a lot of her time had been spent in awe, in newfound appreciation.

She'd had Will on top of her, had been held against his big, strong frame, had felt all of his strength as he'd pounded into her. Seeing it at top speed...

Beautiful.

A little terrifying.

Completely impressive.

Now, though, she'd just finished downloading those mental notes, typing them into her spreadsheets, and was transposing them into the rest of her data and summaries and plans for the future.

The team did a great job of bonding, of coming together—having lots of team events and dinners and meetings, being all in on the sponsored youth program, working willingly with the organization's charity. They laughed and teased and formed long-lasting relationships.

She saw it in the players who were traded and came back to play against the team, interacting positively before or after the games.

She saw it in the hallways and conference rooms.

She saw it in the eyes of her players.

But she also knew a lot of it came from Brit.

She was truly the backbone of the team.

And Brit was retiring at the end of the season. Well, never say never because these players lived and breathed the sport, and the official announcement hadn't been made. But it *was* being talked about in the hallways, and Brit herself had told Lily that retiring was her plan.

Brit wanted to spend time with Stefan and Roxie, wanted to have more kids before she got too old.

So...it was likely going to happen.

And Lily needed to make sure the team would be ready when Brit's stabilizing presence was gone.

So...plans.

Which was something that made Lily happy. Thinking about outcomes and planning for the future, backup plan upon backup plan upon backup plan.

Her soul was singing just thinking about it.

Grinning, she finished typing, was just thinking it was getting late when her phone rang.

A flick at the screen and she smothered a sigh at the caller ID.

She needed to stop avoiding, needed to talk to her parents, needed to move on from the charges being dropped, make them understand she was okay—or would eventually be on that front, anyway.

So, she took the call on speakerphone, her fingers still working on her keyboard.

"Hey, honey!" her mom said cheerfully. "How are you?"

The concern in her mom's voice didn't trigger Lily today, mostly because she was prepared for it and because she was processing the grief of that failure and because...she had Will.

"Great game tonight," her dad boomed, his voice making Lily smile.

"I'm good, Mom," she replied. "And yeah," she said, "the team played great tonight."

"Definitely—"

A knock at her door had her glancing up in time to see the door swing open, Will popping his head in.

"The passing was crisp, and they were working—"

Will winced at the sound of her dad's voice, started to back out.

"It's okay," she mouthed, reaching for her phone, intending to take it off speaker.

"And Will played much better too," her mom said.

"Yup," her dad chimed in. "Nothing like the garbage of the previous weeks."

She gasped. "Mom! Dad!"

Her finger hit the button, turning off the speaker, yanking it up to her ear. "You can't say stuff like that—"

The phone disappeared from her ear, slipped from her fingers, and Will set it back on her desk. "It's okay," he mouthed, dropping a kiss to the top of her head. "Promise." He hit the button to turn on the speaker again.

"Why not?" her dad asked in his usual brusque fashion. "You know it's the truth."

"And," her mom said, "it means that you must be working your magic." A giggle. "These guys and their ups and downs mean job security."

Will perched on the edge of her desk, one ankle crossed over the other, mouth curved.

She bugged her eyes at him, indicating he could go. Heaven forbid her parents say something worse, something that might trigger him, that might fuck with the good they'd begun to develop between them, the good he'd been exhibiting on the ice.

He just picked up her hand, weaving their fingers together, and pressed a kiss to the back of it.

And stayed.

And her parents continued to talk about how badly he'd been playing and how she must be the reason he was doing better.

"He's been working hard," she told them. "It's not all me."

"Just *mostly* her," Will chimed in casually.

She bugged her eyes out at him again.

"Will?" her dad asked.

"What the fuck?" she hissed at him.

"Yeah," Will said, amusement in his tone. "I'm here."

"You played great tonight, honey!" her mom chirped.

"Thanks," Will began. "I—"

"And language, honey," her mom chided Lily, talking right over Will.

"Ah, don't give Lil a hard time," her dad said, talking right over *her*. "She works with hockey players now. You know that means the f-word has become a noun, an adjective, and a verb."

Lil didn't mention that fuck had been in her vocabulary in *all* of those ways far before coming to work for the Gold.

Mostly because her parents were still talking.

"And Will," her mom said, going on like her dad hadn't spoken, "we're not trying to rag on you. We're just glad you're playing better."

"And glad Lily's doing her job," her dad chimed in.

Lil groaned.

Will grinned. "Me too." A beat. "On both fronts."

Her dad chuckled.

Her mom gamely changed the topic. "Well, we don't want to keep you two. We just wanted to make sure you were coming back for our fortieth anniversary party."

Shit.

She'd forgotten about that.

And...she had a ton of work to do, and the team was pushing for the playoffs and—

"I don't really think I can get away at this point in the season," she began.

"She can," Will said.

Lily narrowed her eyes at him.

He let that roll off him like the hot water that had rolled off his skin in the shower they'd shared that morning. "She can take the day off."

"Will," she gritted.

He went on like he hadn't heard her. "And if it's not a game night, I'll invite myself to come along too."

"Great!" her mom exclaimed, "I'll rework the seating chart."

She was going to kill him.

He leaned forward, pressed a kiss to her forehead as her mom prattled on about her plans and whispered, "Party time, pixie."

K.I.L.L.

TWENTY-NINE

WILL

He couldn't deny he was nervous, walking up to Lily's parents' house, their fingers interlaced.

In fact, he was shitting himself.

This was everything he feared, this was him risking blowing up the relationship with people who'd been like parents to him, more parents than his own.

If they didn't think he was worthy of their daughter—

If they didn't want Lily with someone like him—

Fingers tightened on his and he glanced down, stared into pretty hazel eyes. "You know they're going to love how this turned out, right?"

He exhaled.

Another squeeze. "My parents love you," she reminded him, "and they love me. This"—she pointed between her chest and his, toward their hearts, toward *his* heart (that had become hers)—"is making both of us happy," she said softly. "That's where we are and what we're doing and they'll see that, they'll understand that, and they will be happy for us."

"Your dad has hated every man you've ever dated."

She frowned, ear dropping toward her shoulder. "That's not true. He really liked Sam."

Will chuckled and tugged lightly at her hand, drawing her back toward the door. "No, he didn't."

"That's—"

"He told me he knew Sam wouldn't last, so he couldn't be bothered to put up a fuss." Will tugged her a little closer. "That he'd be gone soon enough anyway."

Her eyes went wide. Then she shook her head, bouncing the silken strands of blond hair. "Well, he definitely loved David."

Will snorted. "He thought David was a dumbass."

She gasped, shook her head. "Jeff was super smart."

"And had a stick up his ass about going to a certain Ivy League school he'd attended."

Lil made a face then admitted, "Yeah, that's true, and not that I'd admit it to anyone other than you, but it was a big part of why I broke up with him."

He grinned. "For the record, your dad *and* mom couldn't stand Ashton."

"Oh," Lily said. "Believe me. My mom expressed *that* very clearly." A snort. "Okay, so that leaves Mario—" She paused, tilted her head in the other direction.

"A selfish prick," Will supplied.

Her nose wrinkled. "—and Theo."

"Okay, but still not good enough for you."

"He was an elementary school teacher and volunteered for pet charities in his spare time."

Will drew her against him, getting lost in her—in all the beauty shining through those gorgeous hazel eyes of hers; amusement and exasperation and humor and affection, *more*—for long enough that he had to force himself to focus. "Still not good enough for you."

She sighed, shook her head. Then she rested her hand on his chest, sending his heart beneath it beating faster, his body warming and humming and... "Well, if he tries to say that *you're* not good enough—"

His hand sliding up, drifting over to rest on hers. "Oh, he'll say that."

"Will!"

Lips twitching, he bent, forehead resting against hers for a moment. "I'm fine with that," he told her, and it was the truth— or most of it anyway. "You're their baby, and no person you date will ever be good enough for them."

"You are."

No hesitation, just dropping that bomb on him.

Like it wasn't ricocheting through his insides, sending shrapnel in all directions—warm, fuzzy shrapnel that penetrated every organ, filling him with sunshine instead of injuring.

"Sneaky," he murmured, lips curving.

She rose on tiptoe, mouth coming to a halt a hairsbreadth from his. "I know."

Her lips stretched, curving into a wide smile.

And then she kissed him.

Right as the front door swung open.

He jerked, started to pull away, but Lily's hand had come to his face, fingers weaving into his hair, holding him to her, prolonging the contact.

At least until her mother exclaimed, "I knew it!" and they jerked apart, swiveling to face Lily's mom, who was standing on the threshold, a gleeful expression on her face, her hands pressed together like she was about to start clapping.

Or praying.

Will wasn't sure which.

Because then Lily was stepping toward her mom, wrapping her in a tight hug.

"Lil monster," her mom murmured, hugging her back, kissing her cheek, running her fingers through Lily's hair. "Oh!" she said, pulling away. "Look at your hair. I love those curls! And you!" She spun to Will. "I never get to see you in your suit." A sly glance at

Lily. "Well, I *do* see the pictures on the Gold's TikTok account, but not in person." She moved close, smoothed down the lapel of his suit in a practiced way that tugged at his heart. "You look good, honey."

"Thanks," he managed to squeeze out through a surprisingly tight throat.

"Come in, then," she told him softly, taking his hand and then Lily's, drawing them forward. "I only get you guys for one night, so I'm selfishly soaking up every moment of time I get."

They maneuvered through the front door—somehow, though their success was likely solely due to Val's abilities—then made their way down the hall and into the dining room which was laid out with fancy plates and candles and flowers. Placemats and glitter sprinkled on the tablecloth and name tags that assigned seats.

"Go mingle," she ordered, releasing their hands and nudging them forward. "I just need to check with the caterer."

"Dad caved, huh?" Lily teased.

Val smiled, patted her daughter's cheek. "You know your father would do anything for me." A wink. "Even dress up for a fancy dinner party when he just wanted to get takeout and watch the sun set from a mountaintop."

"Romantic," Lily commented.

"I know." A beat before Val leaned in, mouth curved, voice dropping. "Which is why we're doing it tomorrow."

Both he and Lily laughed.

Val flitted off, though not before pausing at the table and swapping two of the name tags.

Will shook his head, having a feeling exactly which two she'd swapped, but let it go, gaze following Lily as she moved into the family room and followed her mom's order of mingling. The tight red dress she wore was a distraction, lovingly cupping her ass, making him wish the party was over so he could take her back to the hotel and peel it off her.

"You know the only reason I haven't gotten my shotgun is because of the way she looked at you on the porch."

Will blinked, tearing his gaze from Lily and that fine ass, turning to meet the eyes of Lily's dad.

"Don," he said, extending his hand, stomach turning in on itself. "Good to see you."

Don shook his hand, fingers tight, eyes narrowed and sparking. Then his expression cleared, and he took Will's hand. "I hate that she's not my little girl. I know that's not very mature of me and not fair to her. But she's my baby and..." A shake of his head. "I miss that little girl who looked at me like I had all the answers."

"She talks about you both all the time."

Don's expression went stark. "I couldn't protect her."

"You raised her so she can protect herself."

A nod. "Yes," he said softly. "Yes, I did."

Will stepped closer, clasped Don's shoulder. "But that doesn't mean I'm going to stop breaking my back to keep her safe." A breath. "And not just her body, but her mind and heart and soul."

Don swallowed, but his tone was teasing. "That's awfully poetic for a hockey player."

"You threatened me with the shotgun." His mouth turned up. "I've got to pull out all the stops."

A nod, approval in Don's eyes. "Keep doing it for my daughter and we'll be fine."

"Either that or I get Val to hide the bullets."

"You know"—Don clapped him on the shoulder—"you may be the first boyfriend of hers that I'll actually like."

Thirty

She walked out of the practice facility after having said goodbye to Will.

The guys were loading on a bus that would take them to the airport for their next game. More long days and time changes and leaving it all on the ice.

Since she didn't plan on going to all of the away games—unless there was something specific she needed to address with a player—she'd taken advantage of the team being away and had organized some time to spend with the healthy scratches.

Men who lived and breathed hockey, but because of injury or coaching or roster decisions, weren't playing.

Some of those guys—the ones really on the bubble of playing or not—traveled with the team.

The others stayed behind.

And that messed with their heads.

Injuries were tough enough. The frustration of their bodies not doing what they wanted, when they wanted, *how* they wanted ate at them. Especially if it was an injury that had taken them away from the game for an extended period. But she thought the others—those who weren't hurt—had it worse. They were at practice, but not at the games, not contributing.

Or at least that was what Allen thought.

So they'd spent some time together today, and then she'd casually caught up with some of the other men, making mental notes, setting up a time to talk with Charlotte and some of the coaching staff when there was a break in the schedule, and game planning in her office until Will had shown up and they'd grabbed dinner.

But now Will was on the bus on his way to the airport and she was bored and alone and—

Maddy was getting into her own car, her head down and shoulders hunched.

Lily's instincts prickled.

She'd seen Maddy at the bus, hugging Ben goodbye, and knew they were working on their relationship. Had something happened?

Lil hadn't sensed any tension, but then again, she'd been cozied up with Will, no one around them blinking an eye that they were together. Probably because they were wrapped around their own hockey guys, safely tucked away in their yummy player bubbles.

So something could have happened.

And...

"Maddy!" she called as the woman reached her car, yanked at the handle.

Maddy turned around, gave Lil a smile that, even from a distance, she could tell was forced.

Pained.

"Hi, Lily," Maddy called back. "I'm just leave—"

Lily sped up, closing the distance between them, getting near enough to see the hurt etched on Maddy's face. "Are you okay?"

"Yeah. Fine. I'm actually just heading out." Maddy's voice was soft, her eyes sliding away. "It was good to see you, though."

Lil snagged Maddy's wrist when she would have opened her car door, stilling the other woman's motion.

Maddy gasped, flinching violently and yanking against Lily's hold.

Lily immediately let go. "Sorry," she whispered. "I—"

Maddy's throat worked, gaze drifting away. "It's okay. I'm..." She shifted back. "I'm...just going to go."

"Yes, of course." Lily took a step away so Maddy could open the door.

It creaked loudly.

"Sorry," Maddy whispered.

Lil's brows dragged together. "For what?"

"The ear-piercing screech of my door." Maddy shook her head. "I...um...I'm saving up for something a little..." She waved a hand at her car, which seemed like a perfectly acceptable vehicle to Lily's standards. But then again, she'd never given much credence to fancy cars. "...nicer," she finished before her chin came up and her eyes flashed. "And I'm going to do it myself, even *if* Ben keeps trying to buy me something. Even if people think I'm trying to take advantage—"

Words cutting off, her gaze on the trees in the distance.

Then a shaky exhale.

"I get wanting to do things yourself," Lil said into the silence.

Another trembling breath.

"Yeah," Maddy whispered. She glanced back, pulled the door a little wider, started to get in.

"Hey!" Lily blurted.

Maddy froze.

"Do you like fluffy pancakes?"

———

"These are..." Maddy set her fork down, like she had to stop herself because one bite was going to turn into a gorge of the entire plate. "Maybe the best thing I've ever tasted."

Since Lil was right there with her on the gorging—she'd gotten white chocolate raspberry this time and Maddy had picked

Peach Perfection. A stack of wobbly soufflé style pancakes topped with rich dark chocolate, fresh chunks of peaches, and a freeze-dried crumble of the fruit.

Lily was *so* getting that variety next time.

"They are, aren't they?" she agreed, shoving a bite of the raspberry deliciousness into her mouth and very impolitely talking around her food. "I had them one time and I swear, now I can't stop coming back."

Maddy smiled then took another small bite, chewed and swallowed before she replied much more politely than Lily had. "I think I might be a repeat offender myself."

They ate for a few minutes, falling into silence that wasn't exactly uncomfortable, but also wasn't nearly in the vein of content before Lily gave up on relating via books and TV and managed to get Maddy talking about the youth program she was volunteering with.

The other woman's entire demeanor relaxed as she explained she was working at a center that was designed for teenagers and young adults who were struggling with addiction. "I'm not doing much," she told Lily. "I just...sometimes it helps for them to see someone who's been through it and hit rock bottom and hurt the people they love. And honestly"—she pressed her lips together—"they're helping me as much I'm helping them."

"I think you're lucky to have them." Lily reached across the table, intending on touching Maddy's hand, then remembered her aversion to contact, her flinch by the car, and started to draw back.

"No," Maddy said, extending her hand and brushing it over Lily's. "It's just the touch I don't anticipate coming, the ones I can't see or don't expect or—" She picked up her fork, focused on her pancakes.

Lily slowly opened her hand, leaving it palm up on the table.

Offering the contact.

The comfort.

Maddy hesitated for a long moment before she placed her fingers in Lily's, laced them together, lightly squeezed.

"Thank you," she whispered.

"Anytime," Lily whispered back. "But I also think the kids are lucky to have *you*."

Maddy jerked, her head coming up, eyes damp. "I don't know about that."

"I do."

Maddy's fingers flexed and then she pulled back, gaze dropping back to her pancakes. "Thank you." Another whisper, as though if she said it any louder, she might fall apart.

Enough.

Maddy had been pushed enough, had shared enough.

So, Lily began talking about the TV show she used to watch by herself, but now consumed obsessively with Brit and the other trash television consumers on the team. That got Maddy to unlock enough to talk about herself a little more—not just the charity work and the recovery she was putting a lot of work into, but the rest of her.

The woman she was beneath all the trauma.

She loved sports—watching the Gold, obviously, because her brother killed it on the ice, but also football and basketball and baseball.

Fruit was her favorite dessert. Fruit!

And she was gentle, fragile in a way that almost hid the steel skeleton beneath that beautiful exterior, the strength to fight, the mind that was whip-smart.

Not just an addict.

But a delightful woman who worked hard to hide her beauty.

And that didn't work for her, that couldn't be.

Maddy couldn't live thinking she was broken and damaged goods and unworthy.

And Lily wouldn't stop until Maddy saw that she was worthy.

Of understanding.

Of friendship.
Of love.

THIRTY-ONE

Will

Something was off.

Really off and...just fucking *wrong*.

It had begun when he'd slid into bed earlier that morning. Lily had been at his place, in his room like they'd talked about the night before, but she hadn't been asleep like she normally was when he came in at the crack of dawn after an away game.

She'd been awake.

And too damned still.

But she hadn't reacted as he'd moved close, cuddled up to her back, and wrapped his arms around her. Just laid silently, even though he'd called her name and asked if she was all right.

No response, and he hadn't wanted to push at three in the morning. Maybe she was dozing or zoning out or—

It was after three in the morning.

The sky was pitch black.

The house was quiet.

She needed rest.

So, he'd decided to hold her close, let her have that rest.

But now he was awake and the sun was shining through the windows and...she wasn't in bed with him.

Frowning, he tossed back the blankets and moved down the hall, expecting to find her in the kitchen, laptop open, papers spread out all over the counter, surrounding her like little islands of information.

Today, though, she wasn't in the kitchen.

Or soaking in the bathtub, the paperback she was reading covered in soap bubbles.

Or in the family room, playing a round of *Call of Duty.*

She *was* on the back deck, staring out at the sky.

He slid open the door. "Pixie?" he called.

She didn't move, didn't react.

He moved to her, closing the distance between their bodies, taking her hand. "Lil? Sweetheart?"

Still, she didn't move, didn't react to his voice, his touch.

He cupped her jaw, turned her face toward him, and gave her a light shake. "Lily."

She blinked, eyes focusing.

"Hey there, pixie," he murmured. "Glad to have you back."

Will expected her mouth to curve, for her to make some joke about zoning out. Instead, her gaze flicked to him and away. Then she took a step back.

What the *fuck?*

"Sweetheart—"

Another step back, pulling fully from his touch.

"Don't," she whispered.

Okay, seriously, what the *fuck?*

"What's going on?" he asked, digging his toes into the deck, stopping himself from moving forward again, from drawing her into his arms, from yanking her to him...and maybe shaking her until she snapped out of it.

"Nothing." She crossed her arms, glanced back out at the sky.

He gritted his teeth together, forced himself to take a slow, deep breath. "Something's up, pixie," he said. "So why don't you save us both some stress and just talk to me?"

Her shoulders hitched up.

A gentle brush of his knuckles along her arm, wanting her to relax, wanting her to snap out of it. To be his Lily again.

She backed up again.

"Lil."

"Don't," she whispered.

"Don't push you to talk?" he asked. "Or don't touch you?"

"Either." Her throat worked. "Both."

That...hurt. Fucking *hurt*. But he boxed up that hurt and tucked it away. This wasn't the time to let old wounds be ripped open. This wasn't the time to be distracted.

"Tough shit."

She jumped, and maybe it was the tone of his voice—which was harsh—or maybe it was because he moved close again, boxing her in between his body and the railing, both of his hands on the top rail, keeping her close.

Keeping her from escaping.

"Lily."

She closed her eyes, chin lifted, head turned away.

"What the fuck is going on?"

A painful-sounding swallow. "Nothing."

"Bullshit."

Her lips pressed flat, a muscle in her cheek flexing, her eyes clamped shut.

"It's bullshit," he said, "and we can stand here all fucking day pretending that the bullshit is real life, but I think your legs are going to get tired." He stepped even closer. "And both of us are going to be sunburned to shit."

It was winter, but this was California.

The sun was out, there wasn't a cloud in the sky, and he assumed she hadn't stopped to put on sunscreen. He sure as hell hadn't.

"Tomatoes by the end of the day," he added. "Burned, *peeling* tomatoes."

She didn't reply, just kept her eyes closed, her body still.

"Talk to me, sweetheart."

Nothing.

"Did I do something?" He had to have done something, right? Had to have hurt her or upset her or—

Those eyes drifted open. "Do something?"

"Yeah, honey"—he swept a thumb along her jaw—"did I do something? Did someone...did *I* hurt you?"

A blink. "What?"

"Lily," he said, striving for patience. "You need to focus and tell me what's going on, yeah?"

Silence—long, strained (for his part), *heavy* silence between them. There was nothing but the birds in the trees, the rustle of the wind through the leaves, cars in the distance, some kids having the time of their lives somewhere in the distance, their happy yells just barely reaching his ears.

But nothing from Lily.

Nothing from the woman he loved.

And the panic of *that*, of this automaton in front of him instead of Lily, scared him more than the realization of his feelings for her.

Not just protective. Not just affection and caring. Sure as shit not just sex.

This was more.

This was, as he'd told Ben weeks ago, but hadn't really internalized, *everything*.

So, he waited, and when she didn't reply, just did that staring off at nothing bullshit, Will clenched his teeth together, grinding them tightly enough that it sent a bolt of pain along his jaw.

Patience.

But how the fuck could he have patience when she was...

This.

"Lil—"

A blink.

A blip of focus.

Then her stare slid back away again.

And...fuck it.

He lost the hold on his patience, bending down and sweeping her up into her arms, hating that she didn't so much as make a peep of resistance as he carried her to the sliding door and back inside, taking them both to the couch.

He dropped her on the cushions then followed her down, pinning her in place from ankle to chest. "Talk, pixie."

She was blinking again, that focus slipping back in, and her body had gone stiff. *Stayed* stiff as he remained over her, stayed focused as he cupped her jaw and didn't allow her to look away.

She narrowed her eyes, her irises flashing with annoyance.

Thank fuck.

He'd take irritation over apathy every day of the week.

"I can't do this."

"You can't share what's bothering you?" He ran his thumb along her jaw. "Or won't?"

"I can't do *this*." She swallowed. "With you."

That sick feeling in his belly grew. "Can't do *what* with me?"

"This," she said, eyes cooling, body going even more taut. "Be in a relationship with you."

He almost flinched, almost retreated, and maybe he would have a few months ago. But he knew Lily and he knew what they were building. He knew this wasn't right. "Tough shit," he told her. "You can break up with me another time. Not now. Not today. Not with you like this."

"You can't say that," she whispered.

"Why not?"

"Because you're supposed to..."

"Let you fucking suffer about whatever is eating you alive?" he asked, turning her back again when she would have looked away. "Let you help me with *my* hurts but allow your own to continue wounding you? To leave you in pain?" His fingers tightened. "Because I can't do that. I can't be that man. I *can't*."

She exhaled then whispered, "I deserve the pain."

No, she fucking didn't. Not her. Not his Lily. Not—

"Tell me what's going on, pixie." Then he exhaled. "Please."

"It's the day," she finally whispered.

"What day?"

She shook her head.

He cupped the side of her neck, shook her lightly until her eyes came back to his. "Lily, sweetheart. *What* day?"

"The day she killed herself."

THIRTY-TWO

She hadn't realized it was getting close, hadn't really processed the date on the calendar.

Not until she'd been crawling into bed, pausing to plug her phone into the charger and saw the day flash on the top part of her screen.

Then it had hit her like a Mack truck.

Mowing her down in the middle of the street.

And...nothing.

She'd gone blank, lost in those memories, the horror.

The *failure.*

A year.

A year since she'd failed Annabelle, since she'd *lost* her.

"Lily," Will rasped and she realized she was still on the couch, still pinned beneath his big, strong body. "Talk to me, pixie."

God, she'd thought she loved it when he called her sweetheart, but pixie was a hundred times better. Because it was special. It was hers.

It was a gift from him.

But she couldn't look in his big, blue eyes, see the concern etched in his face, the worry and torment, couldn't see it so damned close and tell him *this*.

"Can you..." She blew out a breath. "Can you sit up?" she whispered. "I-I...can't think like this."

A long look, but then he sat up, tugging her up next to him.

"I'm sorry I said..." She waved a hand,

His mouth curved up slightly. "That you can't be in a relationship with me?"

Shit.

She *had* said that.

"I didn't mean it. I—"

His hand covered hers, squeezed lightly. "I know, pixie. I *know*. Now, just...talk to me. Please."

The hurt in his voice sliced deep, agonizingly deep.

But she allowed that to flow over her, sat in it for a moment while she breathed, and then she told him.

About a girl who was bright and lovely and sweet and smart.

About a girl who was talented and worked harder than anyone she'd ever met.

About a girl who lost the light inside her, lost her confidence, lost herself.

And then the world had lost something that was irreplaceable.

How did she tell anyone that?

How could she begin to tell Will about all that was Annabelle, and how much she'd meant to Lily?

She just...did.

"Anna was eleven years old when she came to the training facility," she whispered. "She'd gotten into the sport later than most of the kids on the team, but the latent ability she had was incredible. She was so naturally gifted and—" Lily's voice broke. "It didn't matter. Zack...he has this uncanny ability to sniff out weaknesses, to exploit them, and I don't know if it's because she came to the sport late, so had less practice with mental fortitude and shitty, abusive coaching, or if she was just...vulnerable in a way the other girls weren't." Lil shook her head, eyes burning.

"And the why doesn't matter. Because what *does* is that the abuse happened and because of it, she's not here any longer."

"Lily," he murmured, sliding a hand around the back of her neck and drawing her in.

She didn't deserve the contact, didn't deserve being held against the warm strength of him. Not when she hadn't done anything. Not when she'd waited on the damn sidelines because Annabelle hadn't wanted to get in trouble with Zack.

"You don't understand," she said, pushing away from his chest. "I stood by and I should have done something. But I didn't because she was worried about making Zack even more mad at her, was scared she'd lose her place and—" A tear slid down her cheek. "I didn't protect her. Didn't do my job. Didn't—"

"It wasn't your fault," he said.

She exhaled, more tears falling. "Then whose?" she whispered. "I was there to help them adjust, to keep them focused and make sure they weren't overwhelmed. And she was. She was under such an onslaught that she couldn't take it. So, she took something she *could* control and it's my fault. If I'd done—"

A warm hand drawing her close. "If you'd done what, pixie? What could you have done differently?"

Lily paused. "Everything."

"And would any of that have changed the outcome?"

This is where she struggled. This is where she wondered and hurt and...tried to picture. If she'd confronted Zack, contacted Annabelle's parents, reached out to those in charge of the team, would things have been different?

The last year told her no.

But...that didn't ease the guilt.

"I should have gotten her more help, referred her out to someone who was better equipped. I should have pulled her from the program and—"

Lily stopped.

Pulling her likely wouldn't have helped either. Anna had been living and breathing for the team. Without that to look forward to, she might have ended up in the same place—empty and upset and not here.

Maybe not, but...

"I could have met with her more," she whispered. "Should have."

"Maybe," Will murmured. "Maybe you should have spent more time with her or gotten her in with someone else. Cut her from the team until she was more stable." She absorbed those words like the blows they were, knowing she deserved the lashing, deserved the pain, even though he wasn't saying it maliciously. Just restating her thoughts, her torments. "Maybe if you'd worked harder or found one other puzzle piece, things would be different. But, sweetheart"—his palm came to her cheek, tilting her head up —"she's not here and you can't bring her back."

"No," Lil agreed. "But that means I have to be perfect going forward. I have to make sure that I don't do the same thing again, that I don't miss anything that might—"

"You're not going to be perfect."

Another blow, but this time she wasn't able to hold back her flinch.

"Pixie," he murmured gently. "You *can't* be perfect. And it doesn't matter if you keep working ten-hour days or try to help everyone around you who has a need, or research and think and *plan* into oblivion." He touched her bottom lip. "You'll still never be perfect."

She knew that.

Of course she did.

But...but how could she just accept that?

How could she still be doing what she was doing and not expect to give perfection to the players she was working with?

Because the alternative was...Annabelle.

She couldn't be responsible for something like that, not ever again. And—

"What would you tell me if I expected to be perfect, to make the right call and decision every single time?"

"You can't do that," she admitted.

"Because perfect doesn't exist. Because we should strive for excellence instead—excellence in our effort and in our jobs, in this house and together. But"—a kiss to her forehead—"not perfection, pixie. *Never* perfection. Because that isn't a real thing."

She exhaled, and it was shaky as hell.

Because he was right.

"You're right."

A smile, albeit a small one. "I know, sweetheart."

That startled a laugh from her, albeit a small one. "I wish I could have helped her."

Fingers sliding down, a warm palm cupping the side of her neck. "I know you do." He rested his forehead against hers. "I wish you could have helped her too."

Lily exhaled. "I'm sorry."

"For sharing? For showing me what's inside your heart and mind?"

She nibbled at her bottom lip. "Of course not."

"Then for not being perfect?"

Ugh.

She hated that was kind of the truth.

He smiled again, brushed his mouth over hers so his smile seemed to sink into her soul. "That's the one."

Since he sounded so confident, she didn't agree—just on principle.

Then he sobered. "Can you promise me something?"

She straightened away from him. "Depends."

Fingers flexing, he drew her close again. "Promise me you'll talk to someone about this?"

Her heart squeezed so tightly that she lost all the air in her lungs.

"It doesn't have to be me," he added quickly, probably mistaking her silence, the way her body had gone tense. "It can be anyone who's qualified."

Who's qualified.

Fuck, that squeeze intensified, forcing her to sit in what she'd already discovered.

Her feelings for this man.

Her *love* for him.

"I can get some recommendations or—"

She touched his jaw.

"I promise," she whispered. "I'll talk to someone."

Thirty-Three

"Someone sitting here?"

Lily glanced up, corners of her mouth curving. "I don't know," she said lightly, "what's it to me?"

"One of the cool kids from the front coming to sit next to you?"

She snorted but picked up her tablet and slid to the next seat over.

"Just saying, I was hoping to crawl over you."

Pink on her cheeks. Her eyes hot. But she didn't comment, just leaned close when he sat down, her head resting on his shoulder. "Hi," she murmured.

"Hi," he murmured back, brushing a hand over her hair, the strands catching on the callouses on his palm. "How you doing?"

She sucked in a breath, exhaled it slowly. "I'm okay."

It had been a few days since The Day.

She was...quiet, a little muted, but she was still Lily, still working, still here, still *her*.

And, more importantly, she'd made an appointment with her therapist.

Still, Will was glad she was going on this trip with the team. Ostensibly, she didn't need to travel, but he'd casually pointed Brit in her direction. Their goalie had taken one look at Lil, brought her a chai latte and treats from the kitchen, then had cornered Will in the locker room, demanding to know what he'd done to fuck things up with Lily.

He'd explained—obliquely.

So, she'd made sure Lily would come along for this trip. Where they could *all* keep an eye on her.

Now he was sitting next to his woman, and she was cuddled up next to him, and he was thinking that this, that being here with her, was really fucking nice, even as his mind was curating different ways to make sure it happened more often.

"Now," he said, sliding his hand down to rest on her shoulder, to keep her close, "how are you *really* doing?"

"Will," she softly, "I'm really doing okay."

"Okay as in you need to consume a shit ton of wine and reality TV? Or okay like you just need a little pick me up with a pastry and chai latte?"

Her hand came to his jaw, brushing lightly through his beard. "Okay as in I'm here with you, and even though my heart hurts and I have some work to do, I'm *okay.*"

He covered her hand with his own.

"Okay, pixie."

———

"Beers!" Rome said, setting the pitchers on the table.

Rookie.

Their rookie was officially twenty-one (as of six minutes and twelve seconds before), still a damned baby, but now allowed to drink beer (legally that was) and play a hand of blackjack (also legally).

So, even though they were tired, and even though Will was more than freaking ready to go up to his room with Lily and make use of the king-sized bed, they were down in the hotel bar.

Sitting at a table.

Watching Rome buy his first—but what would definitely *not* be his last—round of beers.

Rebecca was a gem and the team's nutritionist had made sure today was a Cheat Day.

He had no doubt that Rome was going to take advantage of that fact.

To be twenty-one again. Boundless energy. Able to pull all-nighters and not blink, not miss a beat when he got on the ice for the game the next day.

"One glass for you," Rome said, doing the honors and pouring the beers, passing one to Lily. "One for you." Brit. "One for...me." He snagged the glass and sank into his chair. "The rest of you fuckers are on your own."

Brit chuckled.

Lily giggled.

Ben waited until Rome had smugly lifted his glass to his lips then bumped up the bottom, dumping beer onto his face and into his mouth, causing Rome to choke.

And them all to bust up laughing.

Rome sputtered as he lowered the glass, plunked it onto the table, wiping his mouth with the back of his hand and sucking in air until he stopped trying to die via beer and started glaring at them. "Fuckers," he muttered.

"Next time," Lucas said, picking up the pitcher and pouring glasses for the rest of them at the table, "hopefully you'll mind your manners."

Ben smirked, took the glass that was offered.

Axel received his solemnly, though his eyes were filled with laughter.

Will did the same when Lucas held a cup in his direction.

"To Rome," Lily said, lifting her glass to the center of the table. "Cheers."

"Cheers," they all replied, tapping the lips of the glasses and then taking a sip.

"You're nice," Rome muttered, drinking while keeping a careful—and glaring—eye on Ben, but saluting Lily. A slanted glance at Brit. "You're semi-nice."

"Hey!" Brit protested.

Narrowed eyes toward Will, Ben, Axel, and Lucas. "And you all are fuckers."

"I'll have you know," Brit said, "I am nice. Very, *very* nice. In fact, I am *so* nice that I—"

Lily's phone rang and she glanced down at the screen. "Excuse me," she told the table before leaning in to kiss Will's cheek. "My parents," she murmured.

"Want me to come with you?"

He didn't mind drinking a beer with the guys, but if the choice was following Lil out of the restaurant—thus bringing him one step closer to the hotel room—or staying here with these fuckers...well, it wasn't even a choice at all.

"No, honey, I'm good." She swiped a finger over her screen. "Hi, Mom, just a second, okay?" A tap at that screen before she leaned back in murmured in Will's ear. "Also, please save me from finishing this beer." A shudder. "It's awful."

Then she was pushing back her chair, tapping a finger to the screen on her phone again, and moving to a quiet corner of the bar.

Away from the tables of hockey players.

Away from the teasing and shit-giving and boisterous laughter.

Away from him.

He didn't like it but gave her that privacy anyway.

For a little while anyway—long enough to complete the task of finishing both of their beers, which he had to admit, he did in record time, mostly because Brit was expounding on all the ways that she *was* nice.

Very, *very* nice.

"Go," Axel muttered. "While she's in between discussing her prowess in the net and her ability to buy pies from Costco."

Will snorted but didn't dally.

Just pushed up from his seat and slipped away, moving toward that quiet corner, toward his woman.

She smiled and glanced up, leaning into him when he slid an arm around her waist.

"Here," she said softly. "They wanted to say hi to you." A kiss on his cheek. "I'm going to go up to the room and get ready for bed."

"Okay, pixie," he murmured, taking the phone. "Be up soon."

Her smile wasn't as bright as normal.

But it was there.

And that settled him like nothing else had the last few days.

Until he lifted the phone to his ear.

And listened.

Thirty-Four

Lily

The man really had gone above and beyond.

Like *beyond.*

She'd melted down, tried to break up with him, needed extra attention and care and affection for weeks now. Holding her when she got home from therapy crying her eyes out. Stopping by her office and checking in on her. Staying at her apartment, watching crappy shows, and the same sappy movie a dozen times over.

And then, last week, he'd taken her to a small cemetery.

To see a gravestone with a name, a date, embedded in her heart.

There had been more tears then too.

More comfort and checking in on her. The man had even missed a game when she'd had a particularly rough night of it.

"Yes," she whispered, stirring the pan, "because that's what relationships are like, Lil."

She agreed with herself, smart woman that she was.

But she was also well aware that what she and Will were building wasn't what all relationships were like. There wasn't always give or take. There wasn't always support or thoughtfulness or a partner who'd step in instead of walking away.

So, here she was, finally feeling like herself, and for some reason she had decided...

To cook.

Heaven help her. No. Heaven help Will's kitchen.

She'd already burned the bread, nearly sacrificed a kitchen towel to the stovetop gods, and was getting dangerously close to having gone through the backup ingredients she'd brought.

That being, abandoning the fresh ingredients she'd turned into an inedible pile of tasteless mush instead of a delicious home-cooked meal, and turning her focus toward freezer offerings.

She could open the bag, pour the contents into the pan, add a dab of water, and heat.

She thought.

And if she couldn't...

Worst case...pancakes.

She knew he liked those. She knew she could *make* those. She'd bought the ingredients for them too.

It was just...she wanted the meal to be special.

Because...she wanted to...

Well, hell. She loved the man, and she wanted to express that. Out loud, if the time was right and the situation allowed for it. Through her actions, if it didn't. And yeah, her feelings weren't a surprise—*shouldn't* be a surprise anyway. She'd loved Will from the moment he'd walked in through her front door all those years ago.

The difference now was that her feelings, her *love,* wasn't just some silly infatuation.

It was real and embedded deep in her heart, growing through every cell, every muscle and nerve and organ.

She *loved* him.

And she wanted him to know it.

So...cooking.

Silly, huh?

Glancing at the clock, she saw Will was going to be home any moment and quickly stirred the pan. No burning on her watch, thank her very much. She turned down the heat, plopped on the lid, leaving it to simmer for precisely seven-and-a-half minutes. Then she retrieved a couple of—non-disgusting, at least in her opinion—beers from the fridge, plunked them onto the island, and—

The doorbell rang.

She frowned, glancing at the door that led to the garage, as though somehow expecting the sound to have come from there—Will trapped on the other side and a doorbell having magically appeared and—

The doorbell rang again.

"Crap," she muttered, turning the knob on the stove, dialing back the heat. "Do *not* burn," she ordered softly then snagged a towel from near the sink and headed for the front door, wiping her hands as she went.

She peeked through the window at the side of the door, saw a woman in a long flowing dress, gray curls a wild mass that surrounded a beautiful face. The woman lifted a hand, as though she were going to ring the bell again, the many stacked bracelets lined up on her arm glinting in the dimming light of the sunset.

Lil flicked the lock, tugged open the door. "Can I help you?"

The woman froze, blinking in surprise, as though she hadn't expected the door to swing open, even though she'd rang the bell.

Her mouth trembled and her blue eyes went wide.

Bracelets. Hippie-style clothing. Curls. And blue eyes that reminded Lily of—

"I'm Lily," she said softly, extending her hand. "Are you Will's mom?"

"Yes." A beat before she wrapped her fingers around Lily's and squeezed weakly. "Saffron."

Lily froze, not sure what to do with that insertion of a word.

Or herb.

Or—

She released Lily's hand.

"Saffron?"

"Yes, Saffron Eliza Johansson."

Saffron Eliza Johansson?

How was Will just *Will* with a mother whose name was Saffron?

Families were complicated...

Focus. Lily smiled. "It's nice to meet you. I'm Lily Cartwright." A shrug. "Well, Lily *Amelia* Cartwright."

Saffron snapped her fingers, bracelets jingling. "Lily Cartwright. Lily Cartwright. Lily!" She tapped a finger to her mouth. "Now why do I know that name?"

"Because I'm Will's girlfriend?"

"You are?" Saffron frowned. "He hasn't mentioned you." She tilted her head to the side. "Are you related to the Cartwrights he stayed with all those years ago?"

Okay, well, that was...interesting and maybe it stung a little. *More* than a little, considering what she felt for him, what she wanted to tell him. But then again, Will's relationship with his mother was complicated, and *Saffron* was flaky and disconnected and hadn't even come to see him for Christmas, so why would he be dishing to her about who he was dating?

He wouldn't.

Hell, they'd practically spent every day together and she hadn't heard him talking to her at all. Not once.

Meanwhile, her parents spoke to her—and Will—a couple of times per week. Maybe that was too much, but maybe...it meant he knew her parents' names and *they* knew she and Will were together.

Still, this was his mom, and she was here, and—

"Did you want to come—?"

Saffron flitted in through the opening, bumping into Lily and sending her into the doorframe.

"Ouch," she muttered, rubbing her arm as she shut and locked the door.

"Wow!" Saffron exclaimed. "Now, *this* is a kitchen!" Lily hurried back down the hall, moving into the space in question just in time to see Will's mother spinning in a slow circle, as though maybe this was the first time she'd seen the space. And maybe it was, considering all that Lily knew.

"It's gorgeous," Lily agreed.

A sigh. "Although the walls and cabinets are positively dreary." Saffron frowned. "My son. Never one for color. Or inspiration." A slow smile that sat in Lily's stomach like a brick. That smile wasn't...well, it wasn't nice. Not at all.

A slight rumble.

The sound of the garage door sliding open.

"Or artistic talent." A shake of her head that filled Lily's belly with more bricks as Saffron strode through the kitchen and back into the hall, apparently taking her own tour. "And empty walls here? Bah!"

The rumble increased for a moment then cut off.

Will pulling in and then shutting off the engine of his car.

"Pale gray." A sound of disgust that settled another brick on the stack in Lily's belly. "And *white*."

Another soft rumble.

The door from the garage to the kitchen opened and Will walked in, his face lighting up when he saw her standing there. "Hey, pixie," he murmured, moving toward her, taking her arms and drawing her close. A brush of his mouth over hers before he pulled back slightly. "How was your day?"

"Good, but honey—"

He slid his palm down her arm, wove their fingers together. "Whose car is in front of the house?" He frowned, glanced out the window that was over the sink. "It looks like a rental."

"It's your—"

He froze. Sniffed.

"Wait. What's burning?"

THIRTY-FIVE

Lily went stiff in his arms, head jerking toward the stove. "Fuck," she hissed, yanking out of his hold, running to the cooktop and yanking off the lid.

He trailed her, wincing at the blackened, congealed mess that would be hell to scrape off the bottom of the pan.

Eh.

He could buy new pans. Though—

"Why are you cooking, pixie?" he asked, tugging a strand of her hair before he reached past her and flicked the knob, turning off the burner. "I thought we agreed that your specialty was chocolate chip pancakes."

"Yeah, honey," she murmured. "It does. I just wanted to—" A shake of her head. "It doesn't matter, anyway. I—"

"My baby boy!"

He froze, brain not understanding what his ears were clearly hearing.

Because that sounded like—

He turned to the pass-through that led into the hall.

"Your mom is here," she whispered.

"I'm getting that," he whispered back, and after what he'd heard from Don and Val on the night of Rome's birthday—and the fact that his mom hadn't returned a single one of his phone calls or texts since—his mom showing up out of the blue wasn't exactly a happy surprise.

"My baby boy!" she called again, rushing toward him, sweeping him up in her arms, peppering kisses on his cheeks. Her bracelets bit into his back, caught in his hair, but he was good at detangling himself.

Will did so then, embracing her and then avoiding waxing by bracelet when he pulled back. "You met Lily?"

An expression on his mom's face he'd never seen before.

And he didn't like it.

Especially with what Lily's parents had told him.

"I met her."

Cold.

When his mom was normally warm. Flighty and selfish...but *warm* with everyone from complete strangers to his friends.

So, what the fuck was going on?

He brushed his fingers against Lily's, sending her a questioning gaze. Had something happened between them?

Lily shook her head slightly, lifted one shoulder.

"Well," Lily said as she took the pan off the stove, plunked it into the sink. "I should let you two catch up."

"Yes."

A blink.

"Mom," he warned. "Lily—"

"Is fine giving you both some time to talk," she said, rising on tiptoe and pressing a kiss to his cheek. "I've got some work to finish up."

Which was both bullshit and not.

Lily always had work.

But she was here—*cooking*—for a reason.

A reason that clearly wasn't surprising him with his mom.

"Bye now," his mom chirped. "Nice to meet you."

Said in the most *not* nice way.

Lily squeezed his shoulder. "Bye, honey. I'll call you later, yeah?" A glance to his mom. "Bye, Ms. Johansson." Said in a nice way. In *Lily's* way.

Then she was slipping out the door to the garage and he was listening to her car start up and her pulling out.

"Oh, my baby boy, that's smelling absolutely rancid!" his mom said, having made her way over to the sink and sniffing at the pot with the burned dinner all but glued to its bottom. "She can't cook, huh?"

This a question from a woman who'd never cooked for him.

Not once in all of his memories could he recall her cooking for him. He'd always gotten free lunch from school, had eaten dinners at friends' houses or had cereal or sandwiches or something he could make himself.

What Lily had been trying to make for him was almost gourmet in comparison.

"That's not her forte," he admitted, "but she's really smart, Mom, and has a big heart and works hard."

"Hmph," his mom muttered, moving to the fridge and pulling open the door. "Hard work isn't everything."

"Hard work got me here," he told her.

"How do you know she's not using you for your money?"

What the fuck?

No.

"*What the fuck?*" he repeated out loud.

She jumped, blinked, probably because he'd never used that tone of voice with her before. "I'm just trying to look after my baby."

"Since when?" he snapped, finally losing his temper. "Every time I've ever needed you..." He blew out a breath, not wanting to rehash the past, not when it wouldn't get him what he needed.

"I was there for you. Every time you've ever needed me, I was there for you."

That was so fucking ludicrous, he didn't even know how to respond to it.

She thought she'd been there for him?

How could she think that?

"When?" he asked.

Her brows furrowed. "When what?"

"*When* have you been here for me?" he asked. "Certainly not when I wanted to spend the holidays with you or wanted you to come to the Mother-Son game. Or how about my high school graduation? Or when I played my first game in the league?"

"Will—"

"I tried to not hold that against you, tried to understand that you had me young, that you gave up a lot to keep me and that you did it on your own." He shook his head, cranked on the water so that it started filling up the pan. "I understood you deserved to live your own life, so I let that go, let what I *wanted* go." He turned the water off. "But part of me resented it, so for you to come here like this, now, when I'm happy and not lonely for the first time in fucking *ever* and to talk about the woman I love like *that*, to treat her like you did? No, Mom. That's not happening."

"Baby," she said, "I'm just looking after you."

"No, you're not," he snapped. "If you were, you wouldn't have done that podcast and talked about me."

She sucked in a breath.

"Yeah," he said, "I heard about it."

"I'm just proud of you, is all."

"Proud enough to share about my bed-wetting and how I cried when I was cut from the Rockets?"

That breath slid out. "That's part of your journey," she whispered. "It's nothing to be ashamed of."

He ground his teeth together, took his own breath, releasing it just as slowly. "Why are you really here now?"

"I wanted to spend time with you."

"Try again," he said. "The team is heading out on a road trip tomorrow, so I won't even be here."

"Well, are you traveling far? I can always fly to where you're playing."

"You haven't come to a single one of my professional games, and now you're going to follow the team to a new city to watch one?"

"Baby."

"No."

"I love you."

He huffed out a breath. "Sadly, I know that's the truth." A shake of his head. "I just think you love yourself more."

"That's not fair."

"Fair or not"—he crossed his arms, leaned back against the counter—"it's how I feel."

"Will."

Anger prickled through him, a scalding trail through his nerve endings. "Now just...cut the bullshit and tell me why you're really here."

THIRTY-SIX

She shouldn't have left.

Worry had eaten her alive that entire evening and into the next day, ramping up when she called and he didn't pick up, when the only text she received was—

Getting on the plane. Call you later.

Only he hadn't called her later.

He hadn't called her at all.

Now it was forty-eight hours later, and she hadn't gotten anything else.

And the mess he was on the ice...

Told her all she needed to know.

He needed her.

She had to go. *Now.*

So, she packed up her stuff, hustled out of the practice facility, eyes on her phone as she typed frantically, looking for a flight at the same time as she searched in her purse for her keys.

Her fingers grazed the fob—

"Oof!"

"Oh God," Maddy said, "I'm so sorry. I thought you saw me —" She caught Lily's shoulders, steadying her when she started to teeter backward. "Hey, are you okay?"

"I—"

"No," Maddy said. "Stupid question. You're clearly not okay. Tell me what's the matter and how I can help."

***

"Are you sure you'll be okay?"

Lily squeezed Maddy's shoulder. "Yes," she said, even though she wasn't sure at all. Worry was tangling her insides, prompting her with an urgency that made her wish she could teleport herself right in front of Will and *help* him.

She was supposed to help them. Supposed to *love* him.

And...fuck...she'd failed.

She'd left.

"You're not okay," Maddy murmured, glancing over Lily's shoulder at the ticket agent who'd just secured her a flight to Denver. "Is there room on that same flight for another passenger?"

"Oh, no," Lily began, pulling herself together. "You don't have to do that."

"I know I don't," Maddy told her as she passed over her driver's license and credit card, and the agent started typing. "But I'm doing it anyway."

"I should pay for it."

"Hush."

"I—"

"Hush."

Lily bit her lip. "What about your car?"

"It's in short-term parking. It will be good—"

"But that's expensive, especially if you're there for more than a few hours, and with the plane ticket..."

"It's fine, Lil," Maddy said as the agent passed over a boarding pass. "Let's just get you to Denver, get this all sorted out, and then we'll worry about how much they're going charge me for parking, yeah?"

"I'll pay you back."

Maddy dropped her hands onto Lily's shoulders, shook her lightly. "Deep breaths."

"This is too much for you—"

"Did you forget you helped me in the same way not too long ago?"

"An order of fluffy pancakes isn't the same as a plane ride to Denver and crazy parking fees."

"Lil?"

"Yeah?"

Maddy thanked the agent then took her hand, drawing her toward the security line. "Shut up."

———

They made it to the hotel at the same time the team arrived, the big bus taking up most of the circular-shaped driveway, players disembarking and heading into the lobby, getting their keys from one of the interns before getting settled in their rooms, or hanging out in the bar for some post-game grub.

She hurried forward, spotting Lucas in the lobby, not really recognizing that Maddy had slowed down, had put some distance between them.

"Where is he?" she asked, calmer externally now that she'd had the two-and-a-half-hour flight and drive from the airport to get her life together.

Internally, she was a wreck.

Because the first thing Lucas said was, "Thank God you're here."

"Where is he?"

"Nicole will know," he said, waving over the intern. "She's got the room list." His eyes flashed over her shoulder, narrowed and cooled. "What the fuck are you doing here?"

Lily turned, saw that Maddy had approached.

Watched as the other woman, watched as her *friend,* lifted her chin and ignored him. "If you're good, Lil, I'll head home."

"I'm fine." She reached for her purse, extracted her phone. "Can I pay for your flight home?"

Maddy opened her mouth.

"Typical," Lucas snorted.

Maddy's mouth pressed flat, but she didn't look at Lucas, didn't acknowledge the comment. "No, honey," Maddy told her. "I'm good."

Another snort from Lucas, and Lily opened her mouth to tell him to can it, but then Ben was there. "Mads?" he asked. "What are you doing here? Are you okay?"

"I'm fine. I just came out with Lily because she was upset..." she said, allowing him to take her arm and lead her away.

Lil turned back to Lucas, opened her mouth again to tell him to cool it about Maddy, but by then Nicole had come over and was looking at her list, getting the room number and then heading to the front desk for an extra key. Something she returned with in less than a minute.

"Go to him," Lucas said, and Lil knew she needed to prioritize.

Ben had Maddy.

She needed to get to Will.

The elevator was jammed, but the guys made space for her, stepping back to let her off first when they arrived at the floor the team had secured.

Lily hustled down the hall, eyes scanning, getting to his room in record time.

But as she was swiping the key, she realized she wasn't sure how to approach this, wasn't sure what he needed or how to help or what the fuck to do.

Because she wasn't just a therapist.

She was his girlfriend, and he was the man she loved, and she couldn't treat him like a patient, like another one of her athletes.

He meant more.

Which meant that the stakes were higher.

That *this* meant more.

The lock disengaged, the little light above the keypad flashing green.

And she was pushing into the room, heart in her throat, hands shaking, fear twining through her insides.

"Will," she whispered when she moved through the little hall and into the room, seeing he was sitting on the edge of the bed, his back to her. "Honey, are you okay?"

No response.

Right.

She crossed the space between them, perched on the mattress next to him. "Will."

He turned slowly to face her, expression blank, eyes frigid.

Her stomach sank. "Talk to me, baby."

Nothing.

She reached out, settled her hand on his knee, squeezed. "Will, honey, just talk to me."

His big shoulders rose and fell on an inhale, an exhale. "And tell you what?"

Lily held her breath. Then shifted closer and said, "I shouldn't have left."

"No," he whispered, "you shouldn't have."

Fuck.

She braced then asked, "What happened?"

His lips curved into something that resembled a smile— except it was sharp, unamused. "Well, I finally grew a pair and stood up to my mom."

"Will," she breathed, hating the cruel, self-deprecating way he said it.

"Yup, and I knew she was off in her own world, but I didn't realize how delusional she was. How much she had twisted things in her head and—" His teeth clacked together, cutting off the flow of words.

"And what?" she asked after the silence had stretched.

He exhaled. "I can't do this."

"That's okay," she murmured. "We don't have to talk about it now." She shifted closer, reached for the buttons on his shirt. "Why don't we get you comfortable and ready for bed? We can get some rest and—"

"No, I can't do *this*," he said.

She stilled, heart thumping hard. "I can give you some space, honey, but I don't think it's good for you to be alone. Not right now."

He shot up from the bed, paced away to the window, hands fisted and pressed to his hips.

Back to her.

"No," he said. "No, Lil. I can't do *this.*"

THIRTY-SEVEN

WILL

Fuck.

Fuck.

How did he do this? How *could* he do this?

How could he not?

"No, I can't do this," he blurted, the words ripping through his throat.

A long pause.

"I can give you some space, honey, but I don't think it's good for you to be alone. Not right now."

He jumped up from the bed, moved away from her, staring out the window, leaving his back to her, putting distance between them so he didn't grab her, didn't drag her close and tell her everything he'd found out. So he didn't fucking burden her with the shit that wasn't hers to shovel. He shouldn't have started this, shouldn't have gone down this path when she was...*her* and he was him and—

And even so, he watched her reflection in the darkened window, had to dig his toes into his shoes, clench his hands into fists and grind them into his hips.

To stop him from going to her.

To stop this here and now before things got worse, before she got hurt. Or got hurt *more.*

Or—

Fuck.

Just...get it over with.

"No," he forced out. "No, Lil," he rasped. "I can't do *this.*"

He watched her reflection as she straightened on the bed, spine going stiff like she'd just been violently shocked by a current of electricity.

And he knew she was starting to understand.

To get what he was trying to do.

So fucking dumb.

So fucking stupid.

But he had to do it anyway.

"What are you saying?" she asked quietly.

He sucked in a breath, held it long enough for his lungs to start burning, for spots to appear at the edges of his vision. Only then did he exhale, did he brace, did he turn to face her.

"You know what I'm saying, pixie."

Her flinch was...

Maybe the worst thing he'd ever seen.

But she just battened down the hatches, lifted her chin, and took the blow he delivered. He didn't want that. He didn't want to be the person who hurt her, who did it over and over again, and if he continued with this, *like* this, he would.

He'd destroy her.

He'd ruin her.

And...she'd just gotten her life back, was finally happy. He couldn't be a part of taking that away from her, from ruining her future, her—

Fuck, she'd already been through too damned much.

"What are you saying, Will?"

Unable to not look at her, to just take the facsimile of her reflection as this last moment with her, he spun around.

Fuck, that was worse.

Because the hurt had bled into her face, her frame.

She looked as though he'd punched her. Repeatedly.

"You know what I'm saying."

"No," she whispered. "If you're doing this, pulling this shit, then you're going to have to say it straight out. You're going to have to do it. And"—she pushed up to her feet—"you have to know that I'm not going to let you do this."

His heart squeezed. She couldn't fight for him.

He couldn't stand against that.

Couldn't hold firm against it.

"You don't have a choice."

She moved to him, was in front of him in a flash, finger jabbing into his chest. "You don't get to do this. Don't get to pull this shit. You didn't let me get away with it, and I'm sure as shit not going to let you do the same to me. To us."

Her chin was up, eyes flashing, jaw flexing.

Stubborn. Beautiful.

And he had to break her. Ruin that.

"Like I said," he gritted, "you don't have a choice."

"Will," she protested, hand flattening over his chest, over his heart.

Which was pounding like a drum.

And yet, still resolved.

"We're done."

Her face changed, expression flattening, almost hiding her flinch. Not quite, but *almost*. Just like it *almost* eviscerated him.

"That's not going to work for me. Stop. Breathe. Think." She slid her palm up, cupped his jaw. "Any of those. *All* of those. Just take a beat and tell me what happened."

He couldn't.

He *couldn't*.

"Nothing happened," he lied. "Except that I realized that we're not right and we're not going to work."

"You don't mean that." Her eyes glistened.

"I do." More lying. More bracing himself and letting that inner asshole out. "Now cut the tears and move on. This isn't going to happen between us."

"I love you."

Fuck.

Fuck.

She couldn't say that. She *couldn't* say that. Not say *that* and expect him to stay firm, stay standing. Because he loved this woman so much.

It was why he was doing this.

Why he was ending it before it went any further.

Before his shit could bleed over onto hers.

"It's not enough."

Her fingers weaved into his beard, nails biting into his skin, and then her hand dropped and she stepped back.

Thank fuck.

"Why are you doing this?" she whispered. "What happened with your mom?"

Nothing. And everything. And...nothing.

"Are you leaving?" he asked instead of answering that. "Or am I?"

Because he knew that if she knew, she would want to fix it. Fix him. Knew that she'd double down and say it wasn't a big deal. When it *was* a big deal. When it was the only thing he could have ever found out that would have him doing this.

Breaking his heart.

And hers.

"Did you hear me?" she whispered, skittering back another step, her face in stark lines, tears clinging to her lashes. "Did you hear what I said?"

God.

He'd heard her.

And it was destroying him.

"I love—"

He spun away from her, grabbed his jacket that he'd slung

over the desk chair, his wallet and phone from the top of the dresser.

A hand on his arm. The woman he loved at his back, pressing into him. "Will," she pleaded. "Please just wait and talk to me—"

He reached up, covered her hand with his own.

And fuck, he wanted to draw her closer, draw her in front of him. He wanted to wrap his arms around her and hold her close and tell her this was all a misunderstanding, a sick joke, a fucked-up situation and he would fix it.

But he *couldn't* fix it.

So, he peeled her hand off his arm, forced himself to open his fingers, to break the contact.

Her arm dropped.

He stepped clear.

Then moved to the door.

Out the door.

Leaving the woman he loved behind.

He went down the hall, to the stairwell, then climbed to the next floor, walked through the hallway above, knocked on a door whose number he'd noted on Nicole's clipboard.

Knowing he needed to do this.

The handle turned.

The door swung open.

And he stepped inside to accept his destiny.

Thirty-Eight

Lily

She'd waited in that hotel room for a long time.

Until light had begun to filter in through the window.

Waiting for him to come back.

Texting and calling to no response.

Then heading down to the lobby, watching the guys move through the space, waiting for Will to show his face.

She'd corner him, confront him, *make* him tell her what the hell was going on.

She'd given up too easily the night before.

She should have followed him into the hall.

Should have done something else, *said* something else.

But...she'd told him she loved him.

And he'd said it wasn't enough. And...he'd walked away.

That hurt. It felt like rubbing sandpaper over her skin, jabbing her with a hundred tiny needles, forcing her hand into an open flame. And by the time she'd recovered, had shored up her spine and decided that Will could break up with her, he could be done with her, he could tell her that her loving him wasn't enough, but he was also going to level with her.

About everything.

Because he hadn't said he didn't love her.

He'd said it wasn't enough.

So, when the sun had come up and she knew the guys would be getting on the bus, heading to the game, she'd gotten her life—and self—together and went to the lobby.

Where he didn't appear.

He could already be on the bus, but when she'd hopped on and glanced down the length of the interior, she didn't see him, and she didn't want to make it a thing, make it weird for the guys by getting on when that wasn't something she normally did.

Searching row by row for the asshole.

Of course, he was too big to hide amongst the seats. Some part of him would hang out and then she'd spot him and—

No, he hadn't been on the bus.

Nor had he been at the arena. Or at the game. Or in the locker room.

Something Lucas had told her somberly when she'd waited in the hallway, determined to confront him there.

"I-is he okay?" she asked softly.

"Coach says he's fine. That he just had to step away for a game." Lucas leaned a little closer. "I assumed it was something with you guys, hoped he was being a romantic idiot and ferreting you away somewhere." His face sobered. "But it's not that, is it?"

She swallowed. "No," she whispered. "His mom was in town, just showed up out of nowhere. I—well, she clearly wanted some alone time with him, so I left them to it."

"What happened?"

"I don't know." She shoved her hand through her hair, barely resisting the urge to yank it from her scalp. "He went incommunicado and wouldn't talk to me. I saw the game against Seattle last night, knew I had to fly out here, knew I had to see him before he played again and—" Her voice broke. "But when I got to his room, he still wouldn't tell me what was the matter. He just froze me out and said—" She looked away, clearing her throat, jumping slightly when an arm slid around her middle, when she found herself tucked against a big, warm chest.

The *wrong* big, warm chest.

Because it was Rome's.

She hadn't even heard him come up behind her, hadn't seen him step into the hall, but she was really glad that he was holding her so tightly, keeping her together when her hastily slapped-on emotional glue was doing a crap job of preventing her from going to pieces.

"Hey," he murmured. "It'll be okay. Promise."

"Yes," Lucas said, reaching out and brushing his fingers down her arm. "We'll figure it out."

She wasn't sure it *would* be okay, wasn't certain they would figure it out.

They hadn't seen Will the night before, hadn't heard the way he'd talked to her, what was in his expression, his eyes, the lines of his face.

Stark. Determined. *Sad.*

That was what stuck with her, his words, his quiet declaration of her love not being enough.

She'd heard it over and over again.

"You need to sit down."

Lil blinked and turned to see Brit had come into the hall, her face soft, though her words were firm.

"You need to sit down and eat something and then you'll ride with us to the plane."

"I can get my own flight home," she said. "The team wasn't planning on me—"

"Lily," Brit said gently. "I mean this in the nicest of ways"— her chin dropped and she fixed Lily with a stern look—"but don't be stupid." She nodded at an open door. "Sit in there. Get something to eat. Hang out with us until the bus is ready. And then fly on the plane—which has plenty of room on it—back to San Francisco with us, okay?"

"I don't want—"

"Is this where I play Bad Brit and say I don't care what you want?" the other woman asked, still paired with that stern expression.

"I just don't want to inconvenience anyone," Lily said anyway.

Lucas squeezed her fingers. "You're not."

"Hush now," Rome murmured with a squeeze. "We've got you."

"I—"

Rome shifted his hold on her, drawing her to the room, sitting down with her at the table. Brit and Lucas followed and soon there was a plethora of healthy snacks in front of her.

"Eat," Brit ordered and then disappeared. "I'll let them know you'll be on the plane."

"But I can—"

Brit had already gone.

Rome nudged her shoulder. "Better to just let her have her way."

"I'm fine," she whispered. "I promise."

"We know you are," Lucas agreed, though his tone told her he didn't agree with that statement at all.

"We'll just play backup, yeah?" Rome said softly.

Family. Backup. Food and a warm hand around hers. She was supposed to be helping them, but they had *her* back, were keeping *her* together. "You know I'm supposed to be the one looking after you guys."

Brit came in then, eyes gentle. "That's the best thing about this family we've created. There's not one person who has to carry it all."

"Many hands," Lil whispered.

"Exactly," Brit said.

"Except that one of those *many hands* always belongs to Brit," Lucas muttered dryly.

"Damn right it does," Brit said with a grin that had Lily's mouth turning up in response.

"And don't worry," Rome told her, nudging her shoulder. "I'm sure that you'll have plenty to look after"—a tilt of his head toward Lucas—"especially with *that* one on the payroll."

Lucas scowled.

Curses were exchanged.

And then the bus was ready and they were heading to the airport, and eventually, heading home.

And the entire flight, the entire way back to her apartment, she was surrounded by several hockey players.

Unfortunately, none of them was the one she wanted.

———

A knock on her office door the next day had Lily glancing up, a forced smile already in place.

She knew it was a miserably pathetic effort, even though she couldn't actually see it, but she didn't let it go anyway.

And was glad for that when she registered who it was.

"Char," she said, fingers freezing on her keyboard. "Hi."

"Can I come in?" the general manager asked, her tone somber.

Fuck.

Fuck.

Panic coiled in her belly, and she braced, having known this was coming.

Family or not, the back office couldn't keep her around when she was responsible for players not showing up to games.

"Of course." She shut her laptop, waved a hand to the chairs in front of her desk, forcing her tone to remain neutral. "What can I help you with?"

Char slid into the room, shutting the door behind her before her heels clicked across the floor and she sat in one of the chairs.

Sighed.

And then fell silent.

"Char," Lily began. "I get it. I won't make this hard on you. I can—"

Char clicked her tongue, cutting her off.

"Want to clue me in on why Will would come to me asking for a trade?"

THIRTY-NINE

His doorbell rang, a long, loud peel that blearily interrupted his drinking.

His house was dark. His mind suitably numbed.

Wine—Lily's wine. And beer. The beer she'd bought for him that day he'd come home to her cooking for him. He'd finished off the six-pack, and because of that, he had a lovely numb feeling happening in his brain.

Perfect.

He didn't want to feel or think or *feel*.

Thus, the loud blare of the doorbell yanking him out of peaceful oblivion wasn't fucking welcome.

He picked up his beer—bottle seven or maybe eight. Fuck if he knew. He'd been drinking nonstop since he'd left Lily in Denver, since he'd laid the groundwork for what he needed to do and then had caught a commercial flight and come home.

Pack up his shit.

Get his head together.

Harden his heart.

Then—

The doorbell went again, long and loud and totally fucking up his beer consumption.

"Jesus fucking Christ," he muttered, slamming the bottle down onto the table and shoving himself off the couch. "Whoa."

Fuck.

When had the room started spinning?

The walls just cycling around, twisting and turning and...

He sat back down, collapsing into the couch cushions and deciding he couldn't give a fuck about the person ringing his doorbell. And—oh, look—there was the TV remote. He could just turn that baby up a couple of clicks and pretend he didn't hear the bell going a third time.

The remote hit the table.

His fingers—oh, look at *that*—there was his beer.

A bit warm and flat, but it helped with the whole making it so his mind couldn't actually put thoughts together part of his agenda for that day.

Because there was nothing to do but sit there and wait.

For Charlotte to get back to him with a plan.

Beer. TV. Drinking until he passed out.

"What *the fuck* do you think you're doing?"

He blinked, the words sliding through his mind like treacle. Not comprehending because his house was empty and the voice wasn't right.

It sounded like Lily.

And she wasn't going to be here. *Couldn't* be here.

The beer bottle was jerked from his hand, plunked onto the table, foam bubbling up and dripping down the sides.

"Hey!" he snapped.

"Shut up," she growled, kicking the bottom of his foot which —first, *ouch,* and—second, *what the hell?*

He shoved his elbows beneath himself, started to sit up, but there the room went again, rotating rapidly like it was in the outer spiral of a tornado, whipping around, stealing his vision, sending him toppling right beside it.

Or back onto the couch cushions anyway.

"You're drunk."

His head lolled toward the coffee table, the surface covered with empty bottles and his wine glasses. Then back, gaze going to the ceiling. "What gave that away?"

"Such a fucking asshole," she snapped.

"You knew that," he drawled. "I showed it to you enough." A burp. "The airport. Your lush ass in the bathroom. *Shirley.*"

Her inhale was loud, loud enough to draw his eyes from the fascinating pattern of his textured ceiling, draw it to her beautiful face. And God, she was *so* beautiful, so fucking beautiful it took his breath away, made him wish that things could be different.

Actually made his eyes fill with tears.

Fucking alcohol.

This wasn't numb.

This was fucking torture.

More booze. He needed more booze. He turned his head toward the table again, focused, and grabbed for his beer—ignoring the fact that it took him three tries to snag it. Then he brought it toward his mouth—

Lily snatched it from his hand, slammed it onto the table. "The last thing you need is more alcohol."

"It's the *only* thing I need," he muttered, managing to get a hand beneath him, to make it into a semi upright position. Go him.

"The implication being that you don't need me?"

He didn't comment.

Because he might say that he was lying, that the only thing he really needed *was her,* that the thought of her not being here, not being in his life, of her not knowing how much he loved her was torture.

Fucking *torture.*

But he couldn't say any of that.

He *couldn't.*

It would undo everything, make it all have been for nothing.

And he wouldn't be responsible for that—couldn't be.

"I didn't say it," he muttered, pushing up a little farther, reaching for the beer again.

A sigh.

His fingers closed in on the glass bottle.

She snagged it, set it even further away.

"Lily," he muttered.

"Pixie," she countered.

Now he was the one sighing. "Let's just agree to not do this. Haven't we had enough of a scene already?"

"You mean when you walked out after I told you I love you?"

Fuck. Her face when she asked that question.

He turned his eyes away.

"Because I told you I love you and I do—or did or...." She sighed, sank down onto the arm of the couch. "And you pushed me away."

He had. He'd keep doing it too.

He *had* to.

"Just go, Lily," he said, rubbing a hand over his face, the edges of his vision growing darker. "Just go and live your life and...*go.*"

Not the strongest of words, but he was drunk, okay, and it wasn't like he was coherent enough to bust out his thesaurus on his phone.

"First of all, it's *pixie.*" She slid from the arm of the couch onto the cushions next to him. "Second, I'm not leaving without an explanation."

He looked away.

"You *owe* me an explanation, Will."

"I don't owe you anything."

A blip of quiet. "Just...tell me what changed."

"*Nothing* changed."

"What happened between you and your mom?"

His lungs went tight. "Nothing," he croaked.

"Liar."

He was. He was a fucking liar. Part of him didn't even know

why he was clinging to pretending that nothing had changed except his feelings.

The rest he knew he had to keep going.

"We're over."

"You refused to listen to me when I told you the same thing not that long ago," she pointed out.

"This is different."

She reached across him, turned his face so that he had to look at her. And God, that fucking hurt. "Oh?" she asked, almost lightly. "How so?"

Will realized his mistake.

Too much alcohol. Too many feelings. Too much love for this woman who—

"Tell me," she pressed.

Wouldn't give up.

"I can't be with you," he said or maybe begged.

"Why?"

"Because I can't—"

She exhaled, fingers flexing on his cheek. "*Why*, Will? Why can't you be with me?"

"Because—"

"Why?!" she shouted. "Why, Will!? Just tell me—"

"I can't be with you!" he shouted, jerking away from her, the room spinning so rapidly that he could barely discern Lily from the rest of the couch. "I can't *fucking* be with you because she'll tell everyone about you, tell everyone what you did for the girls, and then the media will hear, and your life will be fucked!" He tried to stand and instead fell forward, knees hitting the hardwood, body colliding with the coffee table, knocking bottles and glasses to the floor. "It was bad enough that she was going to make up some sick teenage love story about us and share it, but then she did a painting for the facility and Zack told her some stuff and when you told her your name she put the pieces together—"

He broke off.

But only for a second.

Because then the rest of it erupted out of him.

"And I cannot be the one who's responsible for fucking up your life!"

She gasped. "Will!"

But then the floor was rippling and moving, flying up toward his face.

And the world went black.

FORTY

Lily

She'd called Brit.

And Ben.

And cleaned up glass and spilled alcohol and tried to get Will to wake up while she waited for them to show.

But Will had passed out and he was heavy, and he had a knot the size of an egg on his forehead. Maybe she should have called an ambulance, gotten him into emergency, but when she'd rolled him over, he'd called her name and then had started snoring.

She figured snores were more from alcohol than head injuries.

And the man had a hard head.

Plus, by that time, Brit had arrived with Stefan and Ben had come with Maddy, the latter of which had taken one look at Lily's face and bundled her up into her car then taken her to get some food.

"You need fries," Maddy declared, pulling into Mafia's. "And then once we're full of salt and carbs, we're going for fluffy pancakes."

"Okay," Lily whispered.

"Did you...?" Maddy stopped, shook her head. "You'll tell me over a cocktail, yeah?"

Teeth digging into her cheek, making the inside bleed and throb, Lil forced out a breath. "Yeah."

"Good." She threw the car into park. "Let's go."

They were just pulling open the door when there were footsteps behind them, an arm around Lily's shoulders. "Hey, Doc," Rome said.

She blinked.

Felt her face start to crumple.

"Hey," Rome said softly.

"I'm okay," she whispered.

"She's not," Maddy said, "but she needs a place to sit down, a drink with plenty of alcohol, and a giant basket of fries."

"We can arrange for that." Rome nodded toward the interior of the restaurant. "We already have a booth and food on the way."

"Thanks, Rome," Lily murmured.

"We got you, Doc, remember?"

"Right then," Maddy said softly. "I'll leave you to the guys and circle back to get you in a little while, 'kay?"

Rome threw his other arm around Maddy's shoulders. "Nice try, Mads. You're coming with me. You, too, need a large basket of greasy carbs."

Maddy dragged her heels. "Rome, I'm—"

But he was already shepherding them into the restaurant, dragging them over to the booth.

Where Lucas was scowling at them—or rather, scowling at Maddy.

"What are you doing here?" he snapped when they were within earshot.

Maddy sighed. "Don't worry, Lucifer, I'm not here because I want to spend time with *you*."

"Lucifer. Nice." Rome snorted. "Sit you two." Then he nudged them down into the booth, encouraging them to slide onto the leather bench seat as the waiter came over and handed them menus. That neither of them needed to look at—so they were able to put in their orders right away.

Water and a bacon burger with onion rings for Maddy.

A lychee martini, a teriyaki pineapple burger, and sweet potato fries for Lily, hold the water. And maybe start mixing up the second martini.

Because Lil would need it.

Then the server left, and Lil was at the table with the guys and Maddy and—

"Did you talk to him?" Rome asked gently.

"I went to his house," she admitted, nibbling at her bottom lip. "And barged in using my garage door clicker."

"And?" Maddy asked.

Lucas narrowed his eyes but didn't comment.

"*And* he was blackout drunk, and refused to tell me what's going on."

Rome cursed.

"I kept at him."

"Nice," Maddy said.

"Yeah, you'd think that," Lucas sniped.

"And what?" Maddy asked. "You'd just let your partner cut you off without the least bit of explanation?"

Lucas scowled, but admitted begrudgingly, "No."

Lily decided to just move on. "And he'd drank so much that he eventually passed out, but right before he mentioned that his mom knew something...private about me and was threatening to tell the media."

They froze, Rome and Maddy frowning.

Lucas was the one who cursed this time. "The podcast."

"What?" she asked, brows dragging together.

"Will mentioned that his mom was starting a podcast," Lucas said. "Apparently, listens were low, so it didn't really worry him too much, because she's so flakey about everything and would flit onto the next thing, but"—he glanced up—"is the *private* thing something big?"

"Huge," Lil whispered, the pieces clicking into place, her stomach twisting.

"And he said she found out about it?"

"Yes. Apparently, she did some work for a former boss of mine."

The table went silent. Lily's drink appeared and she took a large, fortifying sip, feeling the alcohol burn down her throat and warm her belly.

Lucas squeezed her hand. "You need to talk to Scarlett"—the team's publicist—"she can loop in Rebecca and the team's attorney and advise you on how to handle this."

"That's a good idea," Maddy murmured, nodding approvingly before she took a sip of her water.

"Did I ask you?" Lucas asked sardonically.

"Are you ten years old?" Maddy countered.

Lucas saluted her with his beer. "Eleven actually."

Maddy sighed, rubbed her forehead "Can't we just put our differences aside and get along for Lily's sake?"

He plunked his glass onto the table. "Why would I want to get along with someone like you?"

Hurt across Maddy's face, but she didn't say anything, just sipped her water.

Lily'd had enough, though. Between Will and the last few days. The worry and hurt and now the fact that she might be media fodder. It was too much. "Be nice to Maddy!" She glared at Lucas. "She's my friend."

"Some friend," he quipped.

Lily clenched her teeth. "She's made mistakes, but so have we all."

He snorted.

"And, look," she snapped, losing the last bit of her temper. "I know you're Ben's friend, and you feel obligated to have his back, but they've made their peace and are working on their relationship, so *this* is the point where we shut up and support them moving forward."

"Lil," Maddy said. "It's okay. Let's just focus on you and Will."

"No, it's not okay." She glowered at Lucas then turned back to Maddy. "You and your brother moving forward is a good thing. For both of you!"

Lucas huffed.

Something Maddy heard too, considering the pained look that crossed her face. "Seriously, babe, it's cool."

"It's not," Lily said, whipping back to Lucas. "Maddy is Ben's sister and they're working on things, so why can't you"—she jabbed a finger in his direction—"be glad for that? Happy Ben means happy teammate means happy *friend!*"

"That's only if it sticks." A shrug. "Because sooner or later, we know where this is going..."

Maddy sucked in a breath.

"Lucas, man," Rome said. "Not cool."

Maddy lifted a hand, waved at the server then turned back to Lily, squeezed her shoulder. "We'll talk later, yeah?"

"Maddy," Lily pleaded. "Just..."

"I need to go," she whispered, eyes glistening. "I *need* to go."

Shit. "Okay," she whispered back.

Maddy's fingers tightened. "Will you be okay?"

"We can go somewhere else," Lil offered. "Get those fluffy pancakes."

"No, really, I'm okay. I just..." A breath, her voice increasing in volume. "I'll let you guys have your dinner and just...have them pack my food to go."

"And probably put it on our tab," Lucas muttered.

Lily's anger was normally a very controlled thing, but Lucas was trying her last nerve. She opened her mouth, ready to snap at him. She didn't get the opportunity to let it loose, though.

Because Maddy beat her to the punch.

"I was a drug addict," she said, shoulders straightening, chin lifting. "*Am* an addict, since it's something I'll live with for the rest of my life." She swallowed hard. "And I stole and cheated and manipulated and took what I shouldn't have. I hurt my brother. I hurt my mom, and I hurt myself. Hell, the list of people I need to make amends to is longer than you are tall. But"—she thumped a hand against her chest—"I'm going to do *it*. I'm going to make things better, and"—her voice dropped—"I know I messed up. I get that. But I'm also working on being someone my brother and mother can be proud of."

Lucas's face changed, expression shifting toward guilt.

Good.

He deserved to feel guilty.

"And I'm going to be someone *I* can be proud of," Maddy whispered.

"Mads—" Lucas began.

She glanced at Rome. "Will you be able to get her home?"

"Yeah, Mads."

"Good," she whispered. A glance at Lily as she stood. "Talk to you tonight?"

Lily nodded. "Yeah, honey."

Maddy moved off to the server.

Lucas started to get up, presumably to follow her, but Rome grabbed his shoulder, shoved him back into the chair. "I think you've done more than e-fucking-nough, asshole."

"Fuck you."

He struggled against Rome's hold.

Rome's hand tightened.

Dirty looks were given.

Curses muttered.

And before blows could be exchanged in the middle of Mafia's, Lil blurted out the piece of information that had sent her on her invasion of Will's house, "Will asked to be traded."

FORTY-ONE

"You're a fucking idiot," Lucas muttered as he walked on one side of Will.

"A *total* fucking idiot," Brit agreed, walking on his other side, the two of them shepherding him in through the door of the youth group Ben had arranged for them to visit a while back.

Will didn't bother replying, just let them lead him in through the door.

Because his head throbbed like a motherfucker and his mouth and throat felt like he'd been lost in the desert for weeks.

Brit had sobered him up and spent the night trying to get his head straightened out.

A fruitless cause.

Because one conversation with his mom had...shattered something inside him. He'd known she was selfish—known it, experienced it, *lived* it. But this was different.

This was malicious.

And it had wounded him somewhere he hadn't even known was vulnerable.

And Lily...*God Lily*—

He couldn't let that happen to her, not when she'd already been through so much. Better she hated him than her life was imploded.

"An idiot," Lucas muttered again after the charity's lead met them in the lobby, gave her spiel, and started leading them down the hall.

"A *fucking* idiot," Brit murmured.

His temper snapped and he stepped in front of them, whipping around to get in their faces. "I get that I'm a fucking idiot, but I'm trying to protect her."

Brit leaned in, eyes flashing. "And how will you do that from another city if Char goes through with the trade your dumbass requested? Huh?"

"I'd be protecting her by leaving."

Brit's teeth clicked together. "Like I said, *fucking* idiot."

"Brit—"

"No," she snapped. "You don't protect the woman you love by not giving her all of the information and then just throwing up walls while requesting that your boss sends you away."

Okay, her putting it that way sounded...

Stupid.

Fucking *stupid*.

But Brit wasn't done. "If she really is a woman you imagine spending the rest of your life with, then that shouldn't even be a question." She stepped closer, got right in his face. "You don't shut out the person you love. You work together because *together* you can do anything."

Her words were...a crosscheck in front of the net, hitting him without warning, sending him sprawling to the ice.

Because was he really going to give up Lily...for a mother he no longer even wanted a relationship with?

Was he really going to give up the family that was the Gold, not for Lily—not really—but for a mother who'd never shown up

unless it was on her terms or because she wanted something or…
because she got something out of it.

Brit exhaled. "Yeah," she told him. "*Exactly.*"

Then she spun back around, hurried over to the director,
Lucas on her heels. "Sorry," he heard her say, "he just needs a
minute."

He needed *more* than a minute.

He needed to go the fuck back in time.

Needed to stop and think and talk to Lily and confide in
her and—

"Oh, sorry," came a soft voice. "Can I just squeeze by?"

Brit and Lucas had left him standing in the hall, his eyes
slammed closed, Brit's words slicing through him, mostly because
of the revelations they'd sent cascading across his mind. Now he
peeled back his lids, saw that Maddy was waiting behind him,
holding a box the size of her—literally it looked like it was the *size
of her*—in her arms.

"Shit, Mads," he said, starting to take it from her. "Just tell me
where to put it."

"I've got it," she told him, stepping back. "This one is bulky
but not heavy."

"You sure?"

A nod. "But if you do really want to put your hockey muscles
to work, the storage room on the end"—she tilted her head to the
right—"has plenty more boxes that need to be moved into the
game room." Another tilt. This time forward and to the left, indicating a door behind him, the one he thought Brit and Lucas had
disappeared through.

"On it," he said, shifting to the side so she could pass him.

"Thanks, Will," she murmured.

At least he could do *something* useful.

Even if that *something* was just carrying boxes.

He moved down the hall, pushed into the room Maddy had
pointed out…

And froze.

Because Lily was there, her back to him, her lush body clad in a T-shirt and jeans, hinting at curves he dreamed about, had once been able to touch. "I've found the other one," she called, presumably thinking he was Maddy, "but it's heavy, so do you want..."

She turned, words trailing off, expression morphing from shock to fury to hurt.

He'd *hurt* her.

And fuck, if that didn't feel like swallowing gravel. "Lily..."

Her eyes narrowed and she shifted the box, leaning it against the wall with a grunt. Then her chin came up, that glare stayed in place, and she moved toward him.

He braced—he'd take a punch, a kick to the balls, a slap—

Only she didn't touch him.

She just...walked by him.

"Pixie—" He turned in time to see her still for a beat, shoulders stiffening, chin dropping toward her chest.

He reached out an arm, his fingers a foot away from her. Then six inches. Then *one* inch.

Then she started moving again, hand catching the door handle, shoulder flexing as she started to turn it—or tried to anyway.

Rattling. *Unsuccessful* rattling.

Her shoulder flexed again. Her soft curse reached his ears.

"Can we talk?"

She spun, glared at him again. "*Now* you want to talk?" A sniff. "And you stooped to locking me in to make it happen?"

His brows drew together. "Lock—" He grasped the handle, tugged at it.

It didn't budge.

He glanced at her then back to the door, as though it would magically unlock. "I didn't—"

A flash of curly brown hair through the small window. A glimpse of a slender-framed woman walking away from the room.

"Maddy," he muttered, trying the handle again.

"What?" Lily pressed close, rising on tiptoe and peering through the window next to him.

He had to physically stop himself from reaching over and lifting her up so she could see better.

And anyway, that was unnecessary because, apparently, she saw enough, leaning closer and calling, "Maddy!"

She dropped her arm, huffed out a surprised breath.

"She just kept walking," Lily whispered, dropping back onto her heels, eyes turning toward him. "Like she didn't hear me calling through the door."

"Or like…" He stepped a little closer. "She was purposely ignoring you?"

Lily's eyes widened and suddenly she was back on her tiptoes, smacking her hand on the wood and hollering, "Madeline Roberts, you'd better get your butt back here and let me out!"

A sigh.

Dropping onto her heels.

"She's not coming back?" he asked.

Lily crossed her arms over her chest. "Apparently not," she muttered.

This was a good thing—for Will anyway. He could show Lil he was done being an idiot—a *fucking* idiot—and—

"Well, since I'm stuck here"—she let her arms fall, took a step away from him—"I might as well finish sorting those—*oof!*"

FORTY-TWO

LILY

One second, her eyes were on the prize—or well, the boxes in the corner of the room that she'd promised Maddy to help with (her payment being one order of fluffy pancakes—of the peach variety).

And the next, she was being swept back against a hard chest, colliding with Will's body with an *"Oof!"* that took her breath away.

"Let me go," she growled, digging into the arm wrapped around her middle, fighting against his hold.

"Nope," he announced, like what he was saying made sense. "Did that once. Not doing it again."

Except, it didn't make the least bit of sense.

He'd pushed her away.

He'd kept secrets from her.

He'd—

Suddenly, she remembered what had infuriated her so completely that she'd invaded his house to yell at him.

"You are *not* going to be traded!" she shouted, arching against him and somehow gaining enough space to turn in the circle of his arm and shove against his chest.

Hard.

"No," he murmured, but she was too pissed to really listen to him—not after all he'd done.

"And you do *not* ask to be traded to protect me." She reached up to shove him again, but she wasn't a physical person, wasn't a woman who went around shoving people...even if she felt strongly that he deserved it—along with a tire iron to the balls. "I can protect myself," she snapped, glaring up at him and focusing on the more important topic at hand. "You went incommunicado. You didn't come to me for help. You didn't even ask me my opinion when the choices you were making were about me, when the choices affected *my* life! Mine!" She thumped a hand against her chest, sighed, the realization she'd come to over the last twenty-four hours settling heavy on her heart and mind. "How can I be with someone who doesn't see me as an equal partner in our lives? How can I be with someone who makes decisions like that without so much as talking to me!"

"Lil," he said, "I messed up."

"You did," she agreed, sighing heavily, hating that her life was her life and that they'd gotten to this point and—

"About the trade," he said, stepping closer.

"You mean about your dumbass request to Charlotte?" she snapped.

One half of his mouth turned up and she hated that she felt that smile in her soul...and between her thighs and—

Nowhere.

Everywhere.

"Yes," he said. "About that. But also about my mom."

That hit Lily straight in the gut. "I—"

"Pixie," he murmured, brushing a hand along her arm, her shoulder. "I fucked up. Big. I..." He spun her in the circle of his arm, turning her to face him. "I'm sorry. I panicked when my mom pulled that shit, not that I just wanted to protect you—because I did and I do—but because...”

His voice broke.

And...her anger melted away.

Because his eyes were damp and his jaw was clenched, gaze pointed over her shoulder.

“It’s oka—”

His palm on her cheek. “It’s not okay. Don’t say that it’s okay, sweetheart. It’s not.” He blew out a breath. “My mom was always...my mom, you know?”

She nodded. “Yeah, honey, I know.”

“And she...the fact that she would risk my job was bad, but the fact that she would risk the woman I love was—”

Lil went still.

Very *very* still.

Okay, she’d suspected, *suspected* his feelings were big, were deep, given how violently he’d pulled them apart to protect her, but...

She hadn’t let herself hope to believe.

“Here’s the thing,” she murmured, cupping his jaw. “I love you. I told you that, and I meant it.” She bit her lip. “I *mean* it, but this has taught me something about myself and the relationship I want and”—a sigh—“I’m sorry to say, but I don’t want to be the coddled princess. It’s already bad enough that my parents act like I’m fragile—”

“You are.”

She lifted a brow.

He winced. “I mean...you’re not fragile like you’re thinking I mean. You’re fragile like the most valuable object I’ve ever been allowed to be in the presence of. You’re smart and funny and talented and good at your job. And you’re beautiful”—he reached out, pressed a palm to her chest, below which her heart pounded —“here.”

“I—” That meant a lot, and his words filled a void inside her she didn’t know existed.

But...it still wasn't enough.

"Thank you," she whispered.

"But," he added softly. "I hear the *but.*"

"Yeah," she told him, "you do." Lips parting, she sucked in a breath, releasing it slow and steady, wanting her words to be careful, measured, *meaningful.*

Instead, they were a blurt.

"I love you, and you told me to leave."

He winced.

"I love you, and you didn't trust me enough to confide in me."

Now his wince was combined with a squeeze of his arm around her middle.

"I love you," she whispered, "and I'm not sure you trust me to take care of myself."

Another squeeze. "Lil."

"I talked to Scarlett."

His eyes went wide.

"She's releasing my statement and setting up interviews."

"*Pixie.*"

"And you can be upset about that or try to stop me." Lil straightened her shoulders and held his gaze. "But it's *my* life and I'm tired of being quiet and hiding in the corner. I didn't do anything for too long and now I'm not going to sit back and—" Her throat went tight.

"And do nothing," he finished for her.

That was it. Exactly. "Yes," she whispered.

"Pixie," he said, drawing her closer. "Don't you see? I'm so fucking proud of you."

She sucked in a breath. Because...he meant it.

She felt that truth in her soul, in the way he looked at her, in the love in his words.

"You're so fucking...*effortless,*" he murmured. "Sliding into the team, accepting them as another extension of your family, and finding all the small ways to help them. Accepting *me*—then and now—and giving me that same kind of care. Hell, even Maddy found a safe, accepting space with you."

Lily exhaled again, pulse pounding in her veins.

"And all of that is because you're amazing and smart and…" His voice cracked. "Your heart, pixie, it's so damned beautiful."

That heart had squeezed tight, was rolling over in her chest, exposing its vulnerable underbelly to this man, but she didn't get the chance to feel scared or hurt or even to form the words swirling in her mind on her tongue.

Because he was still talking.

"I'm not going to say that I'm going to magically stop being a pain in the ass who wants to stand between you and the world, but I *can* promise that I'll stand at your side instead."

Her heart thumped hard.

"And at your back," he added softly.

"Dammit," she whispered.

"What?"

"I want to be mad at you longer." A scowl. "Like a *lot* longer."

His lips tipped up. "Well, so long as you give me another chance to prove how much I love you, then you can keep being mad for as long as you want."

She wanted to smile, but bit it back. "On one condition."

He stilled, expression somber. "Anything."

She should make it on more than one condition, make it clear that she wouldn't tolerate the asshole again, wouldn't stand for someone to treat her like a doll on a shelf who couldn't stand on her two feet, but…

He wasn't perfect. Neither was she.

He would make mistakes. And so would she.

And she'd decided.

On him.

On how she wanted to live the rest of her life.

On what her relationship with this man would look like.

So, there was time to mess up and make up, to be an idiot and an asshole and a bitch. There was time to make mistakes and have fights and movie nights on the couch. Holidays and dinners and time with her family.

There was time.

And they could build the life they wanted.

Together.

Which was why her condition was,

"You owe me fluffy pancakes."

His mouth curved, eyes dancing, hand on her cheek. "You got it, pixie."

EPILOGUE

"Mmm-mmm," she hummed as she took a bite of her pancakes and did her happy fluffy deliciousness dance, the fork's tines sliding from her lips, body doing a little shimmy in her chair.

Spring strawberry.

A new flavor.

And her favorite.

Then again, every single time they added new flavors to the menu, each one became her favorite.

Because...fluffy pancakes.

Because...the man she loved single-handedly kept her in them —or her belly anyway.

"Good, pix?" he asked, smirking over her as he sipped his own sparkling water. No pancakes for the poor, sad hockey player. Today wasn't a Cheat Day, but he'd taken her out for them anyway.

Probably to soothe her period beast that was threatening to murder and dismember all annoying people in her vicinity.

Will was just stacking the bet in his favor.

Doing his best to be out from beneath Queen Flow's laser-like gaze.

She nodded in agreement, but her mouth was curved.

"What?" he asked, clearly noticing her amusement as he smoothed a finger along the outside of her bottom lip, bringing it to his mouth and sucking the strawberry glaze off.

She both felt that between her legs and processed that she was still grinning at the same time. "Nothing," she said. "I'm just happy to be here with you."

"And happy for pancakes."

"Well, that much is obvious." She winked at him as she scooped up another bite, stuffed it in her mouth, then chewed and swallowed before stage whispering, "especially since I'm mostly happy about the pancakes."

A grin.

Then a tug of her hair. "Trouble."

"You like it."

A shrug. "Maybe."

"You *love* it."

Now his grin widened, but he shrugged again. "Maybe."

"How's my poor, beleaguered hockey player doing over there?" she asked a few minutes later, minutes that had mostly been silent because she'd been stuffing her face.

"I'm surviving the torture," he joked.

"Is that why you keep looking over your shoulder?"

His eyes shot back to hers. "I'm right here with you, pixie."

Humor in her belly. "Except for the escape route you're plotting." She didn't mind that he was looking around. It couldn't be fun to be sitting across from her, not indulging in pancake yumminess, waiting for her to finish with her empty calories. She scraped up one last bite of icing and toppings that had slid from her pancakes to sit on the plate and stuffed it into her mouth. "Okay, I'm ready to go—"

Except the words didn't quite make it out of her mouth

because the door to the restaurant swung open and there was a flurry of movement at the entrance and...

Her eyes widened as she saw Leslie, Chelsea, and Veronica walk inside.

"I—"

Will's hand covered hers and she flicked her eyes to his. "They messaged me on my socials after they saw your interview."

An interview she'd done with Will standing in the shadows, having her back while not acting like her shield. An interview she'd done with Maddy, Brit, and Scarlett positioned next to him. An interview that had prompted her parents to visit, pushing in through Will's front door barely a second after it was open and wrapping her in their arms.

Telling her they were proud of her.

With no worry in their eyes.

And...yeah, she hated to admit it, but Saffron's threats were the best thing that could have happened to her.

They'd forced Lily to confront that darkness.

To let it go.

To...do something so she *could* let it go.

But she'd never expected to see her girls again.

"Here you go," the server murmured, setting down several plates on the table, pancakes with all of her favorite flavors, enough to share with the girls.

Who'd spotted her—Chelsea giving a little wave—and were coming over.

And...shit...

What—*how* did she handle this?

She stood up, opened her mouth, and...then three girls were wrapping their arms around Lily and...it was a chaos of apologies (from them and her) and absolutions (from them and her) and then it was the chaos of catching up and everyone talking at once and eating pancakes and it was only long minutes later that she realized Will had moved to another table.

Nearby.

At her shoulder.

At her back.

She caught his eyes as the girls chattered about the results of Lily's interview—how it had finally made them realize that the abuse wasn't worth it. They'd stood up to Zack and the other coaches, had talked to their parents—

It wasn't easy.

But they weren't afraid of hard work.

Will smiled gently, and the fact that he'd given her this chance, this moment of closure, and the space to have it while still being there...

"I love you," she mouthed.

"I know," he mouthed back.

And she *did* know.

Knew that this had sealed a wound she had never believed would properly heal.

Because of Will.

Her eyes stung, but no tears escaped—because of the girls in front of her.

Because of the *future* in front of her.

"And then I tried the visualization technique you taught me," Leslie said, "and it helped so much. My strides improved and my times dropped and..."

She was that girl again.

The one who'd been so excited to come to the training facility, to compete in her sport, to be part of a team was back.

They were *all* back.

And that was the best gift anyone could have ever given her.

———

MADDY, SIX MONTHS LATER

She sighed as she pulled her key from the lock and checked that the door was secure.

Exhaustion filled every single one of her cells, swelling them until they threatened to burst.

Or maybe that was just her head.

Because...the noise.

Good God, the noise tonight had been...

Ear-piercing.

The center's first movie night had been a huge success. They'd been at max capacity, and everyone had behaved, chowing on popcorn and junk food and watching the first in a trilogy of superhero movies.

Everyone had gotten along.

Smiles had abounded.

And she'd been asked no less than a dozen times when the next movie night would be.

So...success.

But God, her ears were still ringing.

Her nephews were loud, but they had nothing on a collective of teenagers hopped up on sugar and fraternizing with their peers.

Still, it felt good.

Not in the blissful numbness that had once been her obsession—seeking, desperate for it, her entire existence reduced to searching for it. Rather, in a tired and fulfilled and proud of something she was doing for once in her life.

Living in the here and now.

In the pain of a sore body and pounding head and tired mind.

And...being okay with that. Not trying to numb it.

Knowing that she'd be okay with a Tylenol.

Knowing that she could sit in her mind and body and be *okay*.

"You're fine," she whispered, turning for the parking lot and her junker. She'd almost saved enough to buy a new—or at least a new to her—car.

Maybe she'd get one with automatic locks.

Smiling to herself, she absently rubbed her head as she walked to her car, dug out her keys, and unlocked the driver's side door.

She pulled at the handle, bent to slide in—

Which was the exact moment that hell broke loose.

A hand landed on her shoulder, and it wasn't heavy, wasn't hard, the grip wasn't painful...but her mind didn't care, her body —remembering all the things she tried to keep buried—just... *reacted.*

"Don't fucking touch me!" she screamed, twisting away, fear making her movements sharp and jerky and *strong.*

The hand disappeared.

"Shit, I'm—"

But the door didn't.

It was right where she'd left it—the heavy steel panel half open. And with her sharp and jerky and *strong* movements, it was right there in her face.

Colliding *with* her face.

She cried out as pain exploded out from her temple, down her jaw, something wet and hot dripping down her face. *Blood* dripping down her face. Her knees hit the pavement, the pain overwhelming her for a moment before she remembered herself, remembered that it was dark and she was alone in the parking lot—

Not alone.

Someone had grabbed her.

She clawed at the doorframe and managed to get to her feet, vision blurry as she scrabbled to pull herself into the front seat.

"Shit, Mads."

That voice.

It penetrated the haze of pain and both soothed the panic inside her and increased it until it swelled up her throat, made it nearly impossible for her to breathe in anything other than short gasps of air. She'd gone still. Frozen. Hell, she *couldn't* move.

He could not be here.

He could not see her like this.

Not her in pieces and hurting and scared.

Not her bleeding and pathetic and—

That hand came to her face and, this time, the touch was

tentative as Lucas lightly gripped her chin and turned her head toward him.

Another curse, his thumb gently running along her jaw.

"I'm so sorry, honey," he murmured.

Then he let her go.

Leaving her alone and bleeding in the driver's seat of her car.

It wasn't the first time she'd found herself in the same situation. She'd deal. She always did.

Wincing, she reached for the keys from where they'd dropped onto the pavement when Lucas had startled her and rotated carefully so that she could insert them into the ignition. Her car rumbled to life. A reach had her head throbbing, but she managed to get her glove box open to extract a stack of napkins, which she pressed to her temple, used to wipe the blood from her jaw.

Good enough.

It hurt, but it didn't seem like it was actively dripping any longer.

Go platelets.

She tossed the napkins onto the passenger's seat, moved to yank her door closed—

A hand caught it.

Her heart skipped a beat, but then Lucas's face appeared in the opening.

He tugged it wider, squatted in the opening. "Let me help you, cupcake," he said, holding up a first aid kit.

She blinked.

Then again when he didn't disappear, when it became suspect that she wasn't actually confused, that this was really happening —the man who hated her viscerally was offering to help her—

She, uh...she didn't react well.

Or, rather, she reacted in typical Maddy fashion.

Imprudently.

She jerked her head back, shoving Lucas away from her as she slammed the door shut. A heartbeat later, she threw her car into *drive* and screeched out of the parking lot.

Leaving Lucas standing next to where she'd been parked, holding that first aid kit.

As she drove off.

Alone.

Because that was what she deserved.

———

Thank you for reading! I hope you loved Will and Lily as much as I did! The next book in the Gold Hockey series is CHANGED. **There was hate. And then there was the love that hid behind it.**

CLICK HERE TO GET CHANGED NOW>

And if you enjoyed CRUSHED, you'll love the bad boys of the Rush! This brand new hockey trilogy begins with BIG PUCK ENERGY. *I played hard, and lived even harder…*

CLICK HERE TO READ BIG PUCK ENERGY NOW>

———

Big Puck Energy

AXEL

I groaned and tried valiantly to open my eyes, but my head was pounding, so the moment light passed my lids, I slammed them closed again.

"Fuck," I muttered, running a hand over my face—

Or trying to.

Because it was impossible.

No, not *impossible*. I frowned, forced my lids open, ignoring the sunlight stabbing at my brain.

Only *one* was impossible because…it was handcuffed to some sort of rail above my head. The other hand was at my side, pinned half under my ass. *That* one was just numb, and I moved it carefully, nerves prickling, tingles shooting up my arm.

What kind of freaky shit had I gotten into last night?

I squinted, trying to remember, but not able to recall anything more than swatches of noise and things breaking and booze going down smoother and smoother.

Until it had tasted like water.

That's probably why it hurt so much to open my eyes today.

A foot kicked mine, and not lightly either.

"Ow," I muttered, glancing up and squinting at the sun. Someone was standing there, not that I could see more than a wavering black silhouette.

"Whatcha doing down there?"

Female.

My mind perked up. My brain focused enough for the wavering shadow to steady, to turn into something…delicious.

Small. Curvy. *Delicious.*

"Depends." I said, curving my lips into the smile that had gotten me pussy from the time I was fifteen. "You coming down here to experience it?"

Silence.

Long and quiet enough that I could hear the birds chirping and the insects buzzing, and seriously, what the fuck time of the day was it?

I hadn't been up this early in…

I couldn't remember. Or maybe I *could* have remembered if the woman standing over me hadn't started laughing. Not a gentle, quiet, tinkling laugh like so many of the puck bunnies that hung at the rink and wanted a piece of me before I hit it big, but a loud and hearty guffaw that shouldn't have been sexy and yet somehow was.

Roughened velvet.

I wanted to fuck her, and I hadn't even seen her face.

But hell, the way the shadows had coalesced into something curvy and petite paired with that sexy unhindered laugh, and I was hard.

"Baby—" I began.

The *click* of a shotgun cocking had my mind rocketing well away from my dick.

Okay, this wasn't nearly as amusing.

Or sexy.

"Hold on a—" I tried.

The laugh had disappeared, taut intensity had surrounded him. "I'm going to talk." Deadly words. "And you're going to speak when I give you permission to do so."

Ice. Orders.

They both began prickling down my nape, curling in my stomach like a poisonous snake prepared to strike.

Meh.

Just call me Steve Irwin.

Of course...there was also that sting ray.

And I had a shotgun pointed at my head.

So...right. I kept my snark locked (albeit loaded, *heh*). The sun, on the other hand, was a total bitch, and since I was tired of squinting against it, I dropped my gaze to my feet.

The woman nudged me with her foot again—this time hard enough to hurt. "I'd advise that you keep your eyes on mine."

"I would," I said, getting frustrated now, that snake darting forward and baring its fangs as I stupidly reached out to grab it, "if I could fucking see you instead of burning my fucking irises by staring into the *sun!*"

Silence.

Shit.

I clenched my teeth against an apology and waited, trying to hold back a wince, expecting the shotgun to go off.

Instead, she surprised me by stepping to the side so that I could look up at her and see something besides blinding white light.

Blinking a few times to steady my vision, I felt my cock get even harder.

Fuck.

She was a porn film come to life.

A cowboy hat on her head, a low-cut white tank covered by a flannel only halfway buttoned up, skintight jeans, and boots.

Not cowboy boots, but sturdy, brown leather boots with bright red laces.

They were well-worn. They were dirty.

They did *not* fit with the curvy little woman in front of me.

"Baby—"

The gun leveled at my chest.

"I don't believe I gave you permission to speak," she gritted out.

Probably, I should shut up, but I'd never been great with authority or people telling me what to do. "I don't believe I asked *you* to wake me up and point a shotgun at me," I snapped.

Slowly, she lifted one hand and tilted back her hat.

That snake coiled again.

Only this time, I could admit it was coiled in the corner in fear, hoping to not be provoked, because it wasn't sure it would survive if it struck again.

"Well," she said lightly, "I normally point shotguns at people who show up unwelcome on my porch, but I *especially* point shotguns at those who show up unwelcome *and* spend their free time tearing up my town." The gun didn't waver, not in the least. "So, what the fuck are you doing here, Axel Finnigan?"

Come to think of it, I didn't *know* what I was doing here.

Last I remembered, I'd been cuddled up to a rather tall blonde and her hands had been sliding beneath the waistband of my jeans.

Had I fucked her?

I couldn't remember.

And it hurt too much when I tried to, so I just let it go. The blonde wouldn't be the first girl I didn't remember sleeping with.

If I was being truthful—something I despised—she also probably wouldn't be the last.

"I don't know," I said, squinting against the sun and trying to actually see where I was. I should also probably be sorting out how I'd become handcuffed to the railing, but...meh.

I'd been in stranger scenarios.

One time I'd woken up floating in a pool, naked, sunburned to hell and precariously perched on one of those inflatable rafts shaped like a giant pineapple. Another time, I'd woken up naked and with half a watermelon (half-eaten to go with the theme) over my junk. Still once more, I'd peeled back my lids and woken up between three nude people—*people* because only two of them female.

The common theme was nakedness.

Yeah, yeah I liked to take off my clothes.

But I had a nice body, and *people* didn't seem to mind.

Not to mention, I grew up in locker rooms, grew up with stall showers where shyness and covering my junk wasn't necessary. I'd seen more dick than most porn stars, but it was part of the game —well, not the game so much as the cleaning up process afterward.

As was the partying and the waking up naked—and sometimes still drunk.

Not much fazed me. Not the dicks or the nakedness or the women and booze. Every time I'd ever woken up in a pesky scenario, I'd just shrugged, dragged my sorry ass out of there and stumbled home.

Sometimes remembering (the watermelon had been a joke by my linemate). Sometimes not (like not remembering if I fucked the blonde from last night).

But I'd never woken up like this.

First, I wasn't clothed.

Second, I was handcuffed.

Third, I was staring down the barrel of gun, the other side

held by a gorgeous woman who appeared to be looking for any excuse to pull the trigger.

"You don't know," she said slowly, as though I were an idiot.

And maybe I was. I hadn't gone to college. I'd barely graduated high school. I was good at exactly three things—hockey, fucking, and drinking.

The middle skill was what prompted my next reply.

"Do you have a bondage fantasy?" I asked, rattling the cuff. "Because I'd be happy to oblige."

The gun dropped further...pointing at my dick.

I watched her finger tighten on the trigger, and I felt fear—*real fear*—for the first time in a long, *long* time.

But I couldn't even push out the request to ask her not to shoot me.

All I *could* do was stand there and watch and cringe and . . . *wait*.

Just when I thought she was definitely going to fire, she spun on her heel, stomped back across the porch, and disappeared into the house.

The door slammed.

And silence descended again.

CLICK HERE TO READ BIG PUCK ENERGY NOW>

———

And don't forget to dive into the the sexy, sweet, and close-knit Breakers Hockey crew. <u>The first book in the series, BROKEN, is now live!</u>
It is sexy, hot, adorable and such a fun read. You will not be able to put this down!" —Amazon Reviewer

———

I so appreciate your help in spreading the word about my books, including sharing with friends! Please leave a review on your favorite book site!

You can also join my Facebook group, the Fabinators, for exclusive giveaways and sneak peeks of future books.

SIGN UP FOR ELISE FABER'S NEWSLETTER HERE: https://www.elisefaber.com/newsletter

———

Hate missing Elise's new releases? Love contests, exclusive excerpts and giveaways?

Then signup for Elise's newsletter here!

www.elisefaber.com/newsletter

———

And join Elise's fan group, the Fabinators (https://www.facebook.com/groups/fabinators) for insider information, sneak peaks at new releases, and fun freebies! Hope to see you there!

———

GOLD HOCKEY SERIES

Gold Hockey **(all stand alone)**
Blocked
Backhand
Boarding
Benched
Breakaway
Breakout
Checked
Coasting
Centered
Charging
Caged
Crashed
A Gold Christmas
Cycled
Caught
Cap
Covered
Crushed
Changed

Coasting

Centered

Charging

Caged

Crashed

A Gold Christmas

Cycled

Caught

Cap

Covered

Crushed

Changed

Breakers Hockey (all stand alone)

<u>Broken</u>

<u>Boldly</u>

<u>Breathless</u>

<u>Ballsy</u>

Rush Hockey Trilogy #1

Big Puck Energy

Filthy Puckboy

So Pucking Over It

Rush Hockey Trilogy #2

Love, Pucks, and Other Stories

All's Fair in Pucks and War

No Pucks Left Behind

Love, Action, Camera (all stand alone)

Dotted Line

Action Shot

Close-Up

End Scene

Meet Cute

***Love After Midnight* (all stand alone)**

Rum And Notes

Virgin Daiquiri

On The Rocks

Sex On The Seats

***Life Sucks Series* (all stand alone)**

Train Wreck

Hot Mess

Dumpster Fire

Clusterf*@k

FUBAR

Perfect Storm

Free Fall

Lost Cause

***Roosevelt Ranch Series* (all stand alone, series complete)**

Disaster at Roosevelt Ranch

Heartbreak at Roosevelt Ranch

Collision at Roosevelt Ranch

Regret at Roosevelt Ranch

Desire at Roosevelt Ranch

***Phoenix Series* (read in order)**

Phoenix Rising

Dark Phoenix

Phoenix Freed

Phoenix: LexTal Chronicles **(rereleasing soon, stand alone, Phoenix world)**

From Ashes

In Flames

To Smoke

KTS Series (all stand alone, series complete)

Riding The Edge

Crossing The Line

Leveling The Field

Scorching The Earth

Cocky Heroes World

Tattooed Troublemaker

About the Author

USA Today bestselling author, Elise Faber, loves chocolate, Star Wars, Harry Potter, and hockey (the order depending on the day and how well her team -- the Sharks! -- are playing). She and her husband also play as much hockey as they can squeeze into their schedules, so much so that their typical date night is spent on the ice. Elise is the mom to two exuberant boys and lives in Northern California. Connect with her in her Facebook group, the Fabinators or find more information about her books at www.elisefaber.com.

facebook.com/elisefaberauthor

amazon.com/author/elisefaber

bookbub.com/profile/elise-faber

instagram.com/elisefaber

tiktok.com/@elisefaberauthor

goodreads.com/elisefaber